"Lorelei…"

It was now or never. If she walked away now she'd regret it. But this was a huge risk; if Donovan turned her down, her humiliation would be everlasting.

Rising up on her toes, until only inches separated them, she dug deep and let the ache inside her force the words out. "I want to know."

Sensations hit her with the force of a hurricane, canceling out her higher brain functions. The feel and taste of Donovan was both new and familiar at the same time, giving reality to what had only been a vague craving before.

His mouth was hot and demanding, each stroke of his tongue licking her like fire and sending sensation searing through her entire body. The solid bulk of his chest pressed against hers, anchoring her to the brick wall at her back and trapping her in a cage of warm male flesh.

It was divine.

This was what she'd been trying to remember. *This* was what her body knew, what her skin had been trying to tell her about. Memories of the sensations butted at her brain, allowing her to savor the anticipation of the next touch, the next taste, while somehow knowing how good it would be at the same time.

"My house is seven blocks from here."

She felt Donovan smile against her temple as his hands splayed across the small of her back to pull her even closer. "Mine's four."

Her decision had been made the moment she touched him, but when he didn't move she realized Donovan must be waiting for a response.

"Sounds good."

Meet Vivi and Lorelai LeBlanc—
these debutantes are Louisiana royalty,
and never far from the glare of the spotlight!

So when they meet two gorgeous men,
it's definitely front-page news…

HEIRESSES IN THE HEADLINES

New Orleans' Most Notorious Sisters!

Follow their sizzling journeys in

The Downfall of a Good Girl
Available February 2013

&

The Taming of a Wild Child
Available March 2013

Don't miss this scorching duet by Kimberley Lang!

THE TAMING OF
A WILD CHILD

BY
KIMBERLY LANG

First published in Great Britain 2013
by Mills & Boon, an imprint of Harlequin (UK) Limited.
Harlequin (UK) Limited, Eton House, 18-24 Paradise Road,
Richmond, Surrey TW9 1SR

© Kimberly Kerr 2013

ISBN: 978 0 263 23435 0

Kimberly Lang hid romance novels behind her textbooks in junior high, and even a Master's programme in English couldn't break her obsession with dashing heroes and happily ever after. A ballet dancer turned English teacher, Kimberly married an electrical engineer and turned her life into an ongoing episode of *When Dilbert Met Frasier*. She and her Darling Geek live in beautiful North Alabama, with their one Amazing Child—who, unfortunately, shows an aptitude for sports.

Visit Kimberly at www.booksbykimberly.com for the latest news—and don't forget to say hi while you're there!

Recent titles by the same author:

REDEMPTION OF A HOLLYWOOD STARLET
THE POWER AND THE GLORY

**Kimberly also writes for Mills & Boon® RIVA™.
Her titles include:**

THE PRIVILEGED AND THE DAMNED
GIRL'S GUIDE TO FLIRTING WITH DANGER

CHAPTER ONE

THE ONLY THING WORSE than waking up naked in a strange bed was realizing there was someone else sleeping in the bed, too.

Someone male.

The bright light on the other side of her eyelids sent pain streaking through Lorelei LaBlanc's head as she tried to piece together exactly what the hell was going on…and who she'd just spent the night with.

She forced herself to lie still; jumping right up might wake her companion, and she didn't want to get straight into a confrontation before she had a handle on things.

Think, Lorelei, think.

She had a hangover that would slay a mule, and it hurt to think. How much champagne had she consumed in the end?

Connor and Vivi's wedding had gone off without a hitch; all of the four hundred guests had had a fabulous time. The church had never looked better, and the hotel had outdone itself with both the decor and the food. She'd been at the head table for dinner, but once the dancing had begun and the champagne had really started flowing… Well, that was where things began to get a little fuzzy. She remembered having a small, good-natured disagreement with Donovan St. James over…

Her eyes flew open.

Oh. My. God.

Bits and pieces of the night before came rushing at her with distressing speed and clarity.

Carefully, so as not to aggravate her hangover, she rolled slowly to her other side. Sure enough, Donovan lay there on his back, bare-chested, with only a sheet covering his hips and one leg. His hands were stacked behind his head as he stared at the ceiling.

She swore under her breath.

"Right there with you, Princess."

The amused sigh in Donovan's voice put her nerves on edge. "What the hell happened last night?"

He had the gall to look pointedly at the tangled sheets—which she was currently trying to pull over herself in a belated attempt at modesty—and raise an eyebrow. She really wasn't ready to go to the whole *we had sex* bit just yet. She cleared her throat. "I mean, how? *Why?*"

"How? Buckets of champagne. And there were tequila shots involved. As for why…" He shrugged. "Beats the hell out of me."

Tequila explained a lot. Jose Cuervo was *not* her friend. *I've done some stupid stuff in my life, but this? With Donovan St. James? And now?* A chill ran down her spine. If she'd *publicly* done something… Oh, her family was really going to kill her this time. Her sister would be first in line.

"Please just tell me we didn't make a scene at the reception," she whispered.

"I don't think so. It's a little blurry, but I think the reception was pretty much over before…"

That alleviated a bit of her immediate worry; being stupid wasn't quite so bad as long as there wasn't an audience for the stupidity. Now, though, she had to face the fact she'd had sex with Donovan St. James.

No red-blooded woman would question her taste. Donovan had poster-boy good looks: deep green eyes, inky black hair with a slight wave that he wore long enough to look a little dangerous, and skin the color of the café au lait she desperately needed to combat this monster hangover. The high cheekbones and square jaw now shadowed with dark stubble spoke to a heritage as mixed as New Orleans itself—if one could pick the best bits and discard the rest.

Donovan definitely rated high on the *hummina* scale. Good looks, though, were pretty much all he had going for him, in her opinion. Why had he even been invited to the wedding? It must have been a professional or courtesy invite. At least a hundred of the guests had fallen into that category. But the St. James family was the worst kind of nouveau riche—using money to buy influence and respectability—and if Donovan had any class at all, he'd have RSVP'd *no* to what had obviously only been a polite gesture.

But money couldn't buy class, that was for sure.

And she'd *slept* with him. She must have reached an astonishingly new level of intoxication to completely lose all her self-respect. *I am never drinking again.*

"Oh, don't look at me like that, Lorelei. I'm not real keen on this new development, either."

Donovan sat up—slowly, she noted, implying his hangover was equally as miserable as hers—and reached for his clothes. Lorelei averted her eyes, but not before she got a good long look at broad shoulders, a trim waist and a very nice, very firm butt. Donovan ticked up another notch on that *hummina* scale before she noticed the red claw marks marring his back.

She'd enjoyed herself, it seemed. Pity she didn't have a better recollection of what had led to those marks. Although she felt like hell, underneath the hangover was a pleasant muscle soreness that spoke to a good time.

The silence felt awkward and uncomfortable. Despite her reputation, Lorelei wasn't an expert on morning-after protocols, but she'd brazen through this somehow. Clutching the sheet to her breasts, she let it trail behind her as she grabbed her dress off the floor and headed for the bathroom. She thought she might have heard a sigh as the door closed behind her.

The sight in the mirror was not pretty. Lorelei splashed water on her face and tried to wipe away the worst of the mascara circles under her eyes. Then she finger-combed her hair until it didn't look quite so wild and made use of the mini-bottle of mouthwash provided by the hotel. Feeling marginally human, she righted her dress and slipped into it.

She could only hope that no one would see her heading back to her room as nothing said *night of debauchery* quite like wearing a cocktail dress before breakfast. Six months of very hard work could be shot all to hell.

Of course she had a much more pressing—and disturbing—problem right outside that door which she had to deal with first.

"Okay," she said to her reflection, "you need a dignified exit." Taking a deep breath, she opened the bathroom door.

Donovan stood by the window, looking out over Canal Street, but he turned once he heard the door open. He'd pulled on a pair of jeans—ending up in your own hotel room instead of someone else's had perks, like clothes—but he'd stopped before adding a shirt. Lorelei had a hard time keeping her eyes from wandering as he wordlessly handed her a bottle of water. She nodded her thanks.

"There's aspirin, too," he said, dodging past her into the bathroom and returning with a bottle. "Care for a couple?"

He shook the bottle, causing her head to throb, and she was pleased to see him wince at the noise, as well.

Lorelei felt like she was in a bad movie. "Look, I think we would both agree that last night should not have happened."

"That's for sure."

She stamped down the remark she wanted to make at that insult. *Dignity.* "So we'll just pretend it didn't happen. I won't mention it to anyone and you won't write about it, okay?"

From the look on Donovan's face, he didn't like the implication, and Lorelei worried that she might have made a tactical error. Donovan had turned his high-school hobby of flaying people alive for sport into a profitable career. He destroyed careers, lives, families. Rumor had it that he was looking for another big story. People tried to avoid pinging onto his radar screen; no one with a shred of self-preservation would bait him intentionally.

"I limit myself to topics of public interest, and even if this fit the definition—which it doesn't—it's not something—*wasn't* anything—to brag about."

Dignity be damned. She was *not* letting that slide by unchallenged. "I wouldn't know. Must not have been that memorable an experience."

"Then forgetting it happened at all won't be a problem for you."

"No, it won't." That was a lie, but Donovan had no way of knowing better, so it was a safe lie. And it allowed her to hold her head up as she gathered the rest of her things.

Her small purse was upside down by the door, her phone, lipstick and room key spilling out. Not far from that was one of her shoes, then Donovan's tie and shoes, then her other shoe. It was a breadcrumb trail of shame that led straight to the king-size bed.

Lord, was there anything less dignified than searching for your underwear? She picked up Donovan's jacket and gave it a shake. Nothing. Dropping to her knees, she looked under the bed. She found an empty condom wrapper, alleviating one of her fears, but finding two more had her cringing.

No sign of her underwear, though.

"If you're looking for these..." Donovan drawled. She looked up to see him dangling her panties from one finger. She bit her tongue and settled for shooting him a dirty look as she jerked them from his hand and tucked them into her purse. The addition of the undergarment, as tiny as it was, was too much for the little bag, and it refused to close. Heat flushing her face, Lorelei had no choice but to take the extra time to put them on.

Funnily enough, she felt a little less flustered once she had. *Underwear was a form of armor, it seemed.*

Squaring her shoulders, she went to the door and examined the fire-safety map posted there. According to the red *X* marking her location as room 712, she could easily get to the fire stairs, go down one floor and she'd come out only a few doors away from her own room. *Excellent.* The chances of running into someone she knew had just decreased exponentially. *Something* might actually go her way this morning.

"Planning your escape route?"

She turned to see Donovan stacking the pillows on the bed into a comfortable back-prop, and then reclining, remote control in hand. He wasn't even looking at her, and, if anything, he now sounded bored. Obviously this was not an out-of-the-ordinary morning for him. *Why am I not surprised?*

"Exactly. Goodbye, Donovan. I hope I don't see you again for a very long time."

She didn't wait for his reply. Cracking the door, she peeked into the hall and found it empty. With at least a hundred of last night's guests having taken advantage of the location to enjoy Connor and Vivi's open bar, she just needed her luck to hold for a few minutes. The quick dash to the stairwell was no problem, and her stiletto heels clacked on the stairs as she moved as fast as possible in the tight skirt. At the door to the sixth floor she paused, took out her room key, and took a deep breath. Another peek showed two people in the hall, but neither of them looked familiar. Just to be safe, she waited until they were at the elevators before making the last break for her door.

Only to find that her stupid key didn't work.

Donovan was relieved Lorelei had left in a huff. He'd been awake for about fifteen minutes before her, and he'd spent that time anticipating a number of equally horrific and awkward scenarios.

But Lorelei had gone straight to indignation and huff—which, in this case, had been more than he'd dared hope for.

Of all the women who'd attended what was arguably the biggest society wedding of the decade, he'd managed to hook up with Lorelei LaBlanc. He'd known both Connor and Vivi at least tangentially since high school and, while they might not be close friends or anything, they were business associates and often traveled in the same social circles now.

He might be considered an interloper by some in those social circles, since his blood wasn't quite as blue as theirs, but no one had the courage to say that to his face anymore. And, while he might not have generations of Old South manners ingrained into him, even *he* knew it was bad form to bed the sister of the bride after the reception.

Yeah, pretending it had never happened was an excellent idea.

Another excellent idea was liberal quantities of aspirin and coffee until he felt human again. That might take days.

The little two-cup coffeemaker on the desk didn't have the best quality coffee included, but it would do for now. He set it to start and the smell of coffee soon filled the room.

The jackhammering behind his eyes had been honestly earned. He'd lost count of the tequila shots, but there might have been a bet involved about who could drink who under the table. He and Lorelei had never been friends, never hung out together, so how they'd got to that point last night was a mystery.

Lorelei had been a couple of years or so behind him in school—and they certainly hadn't traveled in the same circles in those days. St. Katharine's Prep was the school of choice for New Orleans's best families. A safe haven for their precious children from the riff-raff of society, with only a couple of charity-case scholarship students as a nod to "diversity." The Lorelei he remembered had been spoiled, narcissistic and stuck up. Even when he'd morphed from one of those scholarship students to the son of a major donor by his senior year, Lorelei hadn't deigned to give him the time of day.

Oddly, he respected her for *that*. She might be shallow, but she'd proved herself to have slightly more depth than most of her socialite friends when the sudden influx of money into his family's bank account hadn't changed her attitude toward him at all.

Tequila had, though.

He had a few hours before checkout, and the need for a nap was nearly overwhelming, but if he headed on home he could nap in his own bed—a bed that did not now carry the scent of Lorelei's perfume. He might not remember exactly everything that happened last night, but he remembered enough that the light fragrance sent a stab of pure desire through him and made the scratch marks on his back burn. Lorelei certainly had stamina.

He turned on the TV for background noise and picked a news station to listen to while he waited on the coffee. He still had to decide on a topic for Monday's column, and…

The phone rang. Not his phone, but the hotel's phone. Who would be calling him here? "Hello?"

"Open your door and let me back in." The voice was quiet, whispery.

"Who *is* this?"

"Oh, for the love of… How many other women would need to get *back* into your room this morning?"

"Why aren't you in your own room?"

"Because my key won't work." It sounded as if Lorelei was spitting the words through clenched teeth. "I'm now stuck in the stairwell, so will you please open your door and let me in?"

The image of Lorelei hiding in a stairwell caused him to laugh—which then made his head hurt. He heard her sharp intake of breath, followed by some muttering that probably wasn't very flattering to him. It was tempting to leave her there, just for the amusement factor and a much-needed ego-check. But Connor and Vivi might not be happy to hear about that.

He relented. "Come on."

He returned the phone to its cradle and crossed the room. Opening the door, he stuck his head out. A few doors down, he saw Lorelei's dark head do the same. After seeing that the hallway was empty, she sprinted for his door, nearly mowing him down in her haste to get inside. "You could have just knocked, you know."

Lorelei didn't seem to appreciate that statement, shooting him the pissiest look he'd ever seen. "This is a nightmare."

"Just go down to the front desk and they'll recode your key."

It seemed Lorelei had an even pissier look—and this one called him all kinds of names, as well. "I am trying to avoid seeing people." She gestured to her dress. "It's rather obvious that I didn't spend the night in my own room, and I don't want people wondering where I *did* spend it. Or who with."

"Since when do you care?" Lorelei was a LaBlanc. One of the benefits of being a LaBlanc was complete certainty of your place in the food chain. Lorelei could do pretty much whatever she wanted with almost complete impunity. And she had.

"I care. Let's just leave it at that. Just call Housekeeping and ask for towels or something. Whoever brings them will have a master key and can let me into my room."

"That's a lot of assumptions."

"What?"

"I sincerely doubt that any hotel employee who wanted to keep their job would just let you in without a way to verify that you are the registered occupant of the room. And there's no way to do that without going through the front desk."

She looked as if she wanted to argue that point. Did the woman seriously not understand what she was asking?

Lorelei cursed an unladylike blue streak and flopped dramatically on the bed. Then she bounced right back up like the bed was on fire, cheeks flaming.

Honestly, he had to admit it was a good look for Lorelei. The pink tint offset her fair skin and dark hair and called attention to her high cheekbones. Of course he'd be hard-pressed to decide what *wouldn't* be a good look for Lorelei. Even nursing what had to be a massive hangover, she could still stop traffic. There were shadows under those big blue eyes—eyes that were currently shooting daggers at him—but they only emphasized her ethereal, almost fragile-looking bone structure.

That same structure gave her a willowy look, all long and lean, that made her seem taller than she actually was, and the slightly wrinkled cocktail dress she'd worn to the reception last night only made her legs look longer. The memory of those legs wrapped around him…

Lorelei was stronger than she looked. The look of fragile elegance was misleading. There was *nothing* fragile about the personality behind those looks, and Lorelei was pacing now with anger and frustration.

"What the hell am I going to do?"

He sighed and reached for his phone. "Let me call Dave."

"And this Dave can help how?"

"Dave is the head of security here. He'll be able to sort this out. Discreetly, of course."

That stopped her pacing. "You just *happen* to know the head of security for this hotel?"

"Yes." He paused in scrolling for Dave's number and looked up to see her staring at him suspiciously. "Is that a problem?"

"It just seems convenient." She shrugged. "Considering."

"Considering what?"

"Your job. Having an in with security here just seems… Well, *convenient*."

The insult, while not unexpected considering the source, and certainly not the worst he'd heard, still rankled. His columns and commentary were syndicated in newspapers around the country, and he'd built his platform and audience the old-fashioned way. She might not like his style, but he'd earned his place in the national discourse. He didn't need an "in" with anyone to get his leads—hell, these days he had people falling over themselves to provide all the information he needed and then some.

He tossed the phone on the bed. "You know, I don't *have* to do you any favors, and I find myself quickly losing the inclination altogether."

Lorelei's lips pressed together until they disappeared. He could practically see the way she was fighting back a snappy, snarky comeback, but she finally nodded. "You're right. My apologies. Please call your friend."

It was terse, and not completely sincere, but he'd be the bigger person. Accepting the apology at face value, he called Dave. He glossed over the situation as much as he could, trying to avoid mention of Lorelei's name, how she came to be in his room and why she just couldn't go to the front desk like a normal person would in this situation. After some laughter and speculation on Dave's part that Donovan didn't dare relay to Lorelei, he hung up. "Someone from Security will be up with a key to your room shortly. You'll just need to hang out here a little while longer."

"Well, it's not like I have anyplace else to go." She walked over to the small coffeepot and asked, "Do you mind? I feel near death."

"Help yourself."

She did, and then sat in the leather chair. Legs crossed at the ankle, she held the cup with both hands and sipped gratefully. It was an incongruous picture: a disheveled Lorelei, hair rioting around her face and shoulders, in an obviously expensive, though slightly-the-worse-for-wear dress and stiletto heels, sitting primly in his hotel room as if they were politely having tea in the parlor.

And he knew exactly what kind of underwear she had on.

Somehow this was even more awkward than the wake-up-naked-and-get-dressed part. Were they supposed to make small talk now or something? What would an appropriate topic be?

There was small comfort in the fact that Lorelei seemed equally at a loss. He'd bet this situation was not covered in cotillion classes. She studied the art on the wall like it was an Old Master, pondered her coffee like it held the meaning of life, then finally turned her attention to her fingernails. He kept one eye on the TV and feigned interest in the talking heads on the morning show. He'd made his living by always having something to say, but this time his vaunted golden tongue failed him.

Lorelei cleared her throat. "So, will you be writing about the wedding?"

Lord, she really had no idea what he did for a living. "I don't do society news, Lorelei. I came as a guest to the wedding, nothing more."

"I had no idea you'd become such good friends with Connor and Vivi."

"I sit on two boards with Vivi. We share an interest in the arts. Connor and I have several mutual friends. I wouldn't exactly call us close, but I probably know them at least as well as a third of that guest list."

"They are a popular couple."

"Indeed."

"And it was an amazing event, start to finish."

It had been a star-studded event, thanks to Connor's fame, and the entire ranks of the New Orleans elite had been there, traveling in their usual pack. "I expected nothing less."

Lorelei nodded, and he realized that topic had now run its course. Well, that had killed a couple of minutes. How long would it take Security to bring Lorelei a key?

She seemed to be wondering the same thing. "I wish they'd hurry."

"Me, too. I have things I need to do."

"Well, don't let me stop you."

His three options were to take a shower, take a nap or go home—none of which he could do while Lorelei was parked in his room. "I'm sure they'll be here shortly."

Hard on those words there was a knock at the door, and Lorelei jumped up as he went to answer it. Her sigh of relief when the man identified himself as the assistant head of security was audible from across the room. He asked to see her ID, verified her as the occupant of the room, then handed her a key. "Would you like me to escort you to your room, miss?"

"No!" she practically shouted, before she caught herself and lowered her voice. "I'll be fine, thank you."

The man nodded, then left without question, and Donovan wondered exactly what Dave had told him about his assignment. Of course it probably wasn't the oddest thing Security had ever done: this hotel catered to an elite crowd, and that elite had probably made far more questionable requests of Security in the past. He'd moved more toward analysis and away from the "shocking exposé" camp of journalism himself, but he'd bet there were all kinds of stories to be told from this hotel.

Lorelei cleared her throat, bringing him back to his own little drama. "Goodbye. Again. Thank you for your assistance, and, um, have a nice life."

The re-do of her exit lacked the dramatic huff this time,

but it retained its silliness as Lorelei once again checked the hall and slipped out like a bumbling spy in a bad movie.

At least he knew she wouldn't be back this time. Oddly, that seemed to be a little of a letdown. Lorelei certainly had entertainment value.

Although he'd been thinking more about the events of the morning, not last night, another particularly *entertaining* visual flashed across his mind.

And that quickly answered his question about what he'd do now: a cold shower was calling his name.

CHAPTER TWO

A GUILTY CONSCIENCE was a terrible thing. It wasn't something Lorelei was overly familiar with, as she intentionally kept away from situations that might lead to one. She had regrets, sure, but she'd always lived—well, until recently—by the philosophy that she'd rather regret the things she'd done than regret that she'd never done them at all. So why did this thing with Donovan seem to be haunting her?

It wasn't even worry over what people might say. As far as she could tell, no one knew. Vivi and Connor had left for their honeymoon and Vivi hadn't said a word. She'd waited on pins and needles for the news to circulate, but it seemed she was going to get away with it. She'd gotten lucky by not screwing the whole plan up at the eleventh hour.

So the worry had to be over Donovan himself.

Over the last three days, more of her memory had returned—but not the parts she'd have liked. If she *had* to carry around the knowledge that she'd had sex with Donovan St. James, she'd like to be in possession of memories of the good stuff, too. She had all the knowledge she needed to know that she'd enjoyed herself, but she lacked the memory of the proof. It seemed like a shame.

She rolled over and punched her pillow into shape.

Vague, incomplete dreams were leaving her tired and grouchy in the mornings and, even worse, leaving her with a ghostly, frustrated feeling.

Maybe that was why she couldn't quite shake the whole situation off: she wanted that memory and her brain was determined to wring out the tequila and find it. Maybe she wasn't feeling guilty; maybe she was just confusing one nagging feeling with another.

And now she had to be hallucinating, because she could *hear* Donovan's voice. She sat up. That wasn't a hallucination; that really was Donovan's voice, coming from her living room. *What the hell?* Shock rocketed through her as she heaved herself out of bed, covers flying. She was in the hallway before she caught herself in the middle of the ridiculous thought.

It was coming from the TV.

"Morning." Callie sat on the couch, hugging a cup of coffee and watching the morning news. She was dressed already, her backpack on the coffee table, ready to go.

Although this was technically still Vivi's house, Vivi had moved out six months ago, after news of her engagement to Connor hit the press. The little house on Frenchman Street just couldn't provide the privacy and security Connor and Vivi needed. Lorelei had enjoyed the solitude for about two weeks, but had then offered Vivi's old room to a friend-of-a-friend just so she'd have some company.

It hadn't quite worked. Between Callie's schedule and her latest romance with some guy she'd met at the library, she was rarely home. It was only slightly better than living alone.

Callie was a news junkie—the serious stuff, not the pop-culture and human-interest fluff—and now Donovan's face filled the screen as he droned on about something being unconstitutional. Callie was rapturously hanging on every word, and Lorelei wondered if it was because anything unconstitutional was catnip for Loyola Law students or because the words were coming out of Donovan's pretty face.

Lorelei wished she'd purchased a smaller, lower-quality TV, because the sight of Donovan in HD sent a jolt through her. She tried to brush it away and act casual as she continued to the kitchen and the coffeepot. She moved in slow motion, killing time, but Donovan was *still* talking—no surprise there, really; the man truly loved to hear himself talk. Finally she couldn't stall any longer and had to go back out into the living room.

"No class today?" she asked as she took the other corner of the couch and settled in.

"The air-conditioning in the building is broken. They had to cancel classes."

Lorelei nodded. The older buildings in New Orleans— those built before the invention of air-conditioning and designed for the heat—could sometimes be habitable, if not comfortable, in August, but not the newer buildings, with their low ceilings and windowless rooms.

"I'm meeting my study group at the library instead. What about you? Not going to the studio?"

"With Connor away, things are pretty slow at the moment. I'll go in later and check messages and things, but a vacation for the boss is a vacation for the minions, as well."

People might think that Connor had hired her as assistant and office manager for ConMan Studios out of pure nepotism—and that did have a little to do with it—but the truth was she was good at the job, much to everyone's surprise. She'd finally started to earn a little respect; somehow her working for her brother-in-law impressed people more than just working for her father, even though the positions were very similar.

And she liked it, too. Who wouldn't want to be part of a rock star's entourage? It was exciting, and the high-profile nature of the job meant people knew she was actually earning her keep.

"I'm kind of glad things will be slow. Being Vivi for the next three weeks is going to be crazy enough."

Callie nodded, but she wasn't really listening. She still had most of her attention on the TV—where, thankfully, Donovan was wrapping up. "Donovan St. James is right. The city is just asking for a major lawsuit."

Lorelei didn't bother to ask about what. "I've always wondered how someone becomes a pundit," she said in what she hoped sounded like idle curiosity. "Is there a degree program for that? A Bachelor's in Talking Headism?"

Callie shrugged. "I think you just have to make a name for yourself in politics or journalism to prove that you're smart enough to have something sensible to say, and then show that you're articulate enough to say it on TV."

"Then how did Donovan St. James get anointed?"

Callie looked at her like she was crazy. "Because he's freaking *brilliant*."

"So *you* say."

"No, so says the world. Haven't you ever read his column?"

"Not since he destroyed the DuBois and Dillard families."

"They brought that on themselves. Corruption tends to bite you in the butt like that when it's uncovered."

Lorelei had sympathy for her friends' families. It had rocked everyone's world. "But Donovan seemed to *enjoy* it. He certainly got a lot of attention out of their misery."

"That *is* what got him attention initially. But in the

last three years that attention has grown because of his insightful analysis and dogged chasing of facts. When he comments on politics and issues, people listen. He's syndicated in newspapers and on websites all over the country. That's why he's on TV all the time."

"Oh. I didn't know that." Hmm, it seemed she should have.

"Now you do. Should you decide to get more up-to-date on the rest of the world, his columns wouldn't be a bad place to start. There's an archive on his website. Good stuff there. I've even quoted him in some of my papers."

Well, it seemed that Donovan had been out making a name for himself over the years and she'd been ignorant of the whole thing. Callie didn't need to look so darn surprised. Just because she used to go to school with Donovan, it didn't mean she was an expert on his life—or that she wanted to be.

Politics—and the blow-hard talking heads that covered it—gave her a headache. The news depressed her. She heard enough from Callie to keep her feeling at least as well-informed as the average citizen; she didn't need to go looking for more than that.

Callie tossed the remote her way and grabbed her backpack. "I'm gone. Some of us might go grab some drinks after we're done with study group. Want to come?"

"Thanks, but not tonight." Her personal prohibition was still in place—the memory of Sunday morning was still too fresh even to consider breaking it.

"Call me if you change your mind. Bye."

"Bye."

A second later Callie reappeared. "Today's paper." She tossed it on the coffee table. "By the way, Donovan's column runs in the editorial section—if you're interested, that is."

Once Callie had left, Lorelei unrolled the paper, flipped to the middle and pulled out what her grandmother and mother still called the "Wednesday Pages," even though it was now a glossy, magazine-style insert about society's doings. There, on the cover, was a full-color picture of Vivi and Connor on their way out of the cathedral. The caption promised a full write-up and more pictures inside. Lorelei flipped to the pages. There were some great shots of the guests going into the church, and a few from the reception. Most of them focused on the star-studded guest list of Connor's friends in the music business, but there were a few photos of New Orleans' business and society leaders. She had made the cut, too, in a photo of the bridesmaids and Mom and Dad with Vivi, right before they went into the church. Donovan was in a picture as well, standing in a group with some city councilmen and the heads of three charitable organizations Vivi worked with.

The picture of Donovan made her think of Callie's parting shot, and she flipped to the editorial section to find his opinion of a bill being argued in Congress this week. It seemed well-written and impressive in its commentary, but she'd need a primer about the bill itself before she could form a cogent opinion.

Lord, even his writing had that condescending, sarcastic tone. Donovan had a hell of a chip on his shoulder.

She folded the newspaper decisively. Time to shake off this whole Donovan thing and move on. Forget it ever happened. She'd go to the studio, get some work done, maybe meet Callie for dinner, if not drinks. She needed to look over Vivi's schedule, start preparing herself and firm up her plan of action. She would take center stage tomorrow. Her first big appearance in her new temporary role.

Butterflies battered her insides. It was stage fright—but not because she would be center stage. This was make or break time. If she screwed this up, she'd only prove to everyone that she really was a flaky screw-up, an airhead with only her trust fund going for her. But if it went well... She sighed. If it went well she'd be on her way—not just "the other LaBlanc girl" anymore. The last six months had been building toward this moment, and the pressure was doing bad things to her.

It was just one more reason why she needed to forget about what happened with Donovan and focus on what was important. Staying busy was a very good idea; it would give her mind something to think about other than Donovan, and soon enough she'd be past this whole embarrassing situation.

She picked up her coffee cup and the society section again, intending to set it aside for Vivi, when her own name caught her eye.

Several of the younger guests continued the celebrations long into the night, keeping the bar open and the staff hopping. Lorelei LaBlanc, sister of the bride and Maid of Honor, swapped her bridesmaid's dress for a flirty, sparkly number and danced the night away with some of the city's most eligible bachelors. Interestingly, she and the most eligible bachelor of all, journalist and TV commentator Donovan St. James, seemed to be quite friendly—much to the dismay of the other eligible bachelors and bachelorettes.

Lorelei nearly dropped her coffee.
Oh, merde.

St. James Media looked like any average office building from the outside, but within the company the building was called "Whiz Castle." It had been built on the success of an infomercial for the unfortunately named Toilet Whiz, which had taken the company from struggling to superstar nearly overnight and made them the largest direct response and infomercial production company in the South. His father had an original Toilet Whiz framed and hanging outside Studio One in a place of honor.

The sight still made Donovan laugh every time he passed it. Part of Donovan's success as a TV personality came from the fact he always seemed to be amused about something when the cameras rolled; only a few people knew it was because he'd just passed a framed Toilet Whiz.

Donovan had an office right down the hall from his father's, but he rarely used it. He wasn't a part of the business—infomercials had given him a comfortable checking-account balance and paid his college tuition, but he wasn't interested in the actual production of them—but since his siblings had offices in the building Dad had given him one, too.

He could have used it, but he far preferred to work in his own space, where there were fewer distractions and his tendency to work odd hours went unquestioned. Because he was so rarely there, his office had a sterile, unlived-in feeling. It was expertly and expensively decorated, and it gave him a place to hang plaques and pictures and things, but he couldn't actually work in there.

He was using the studios more often these days, though, as his TV appearance schedule picked up. Their facilities and staff were truly top-notch, and he'd found he rather liked using the family's home field. His brothers had even expanded the studio's capabilities, and St. James Media was getting traffic from a lot of famous faces these days.

Maybe he *had* contributed something to the family business, after all.

However, it was proving quite handy to have the office to use as a place to drop off his stuff and put on a tie before he went on air. Unknotting the noose around his neck, he headed back toward his office, ready to go home.

His father's secretary followed him down the long hallway, talking a mile a minute, and he listened with half an ear. As he opened his office door and saw Lorelei sitting on the low sofa under the window, he wished he'd paid a bit more attention.

How had she known he'd be here?

He closed the door behind him. "Lorelei. This is… unexpected."

She crossed her arms over her chest. "Oh, really?" Sarcasm dripped off her words.

"Yeah. Your 'have a nice life' statement kind of implied you wouldn't be dropping by to chat."

"That was before we made the newspaper."

"We?"

"Yes, *we.*" She sounded downright irritated about it.

"When? For what?"

"This morning. In the write-up about the wedding."

"And you came by to tell me about it?"

"I rather assumed you'd already know."

This was obviously going to take more than just a minute. He sat on the edge of his desk. "Uh, no. I usually skip that part of the paper."

"Well, it might not be as far-reaching as that transportation bill, but it certainly rocks *this* little part of the world."

The mention of his column caught him off-guard. He wouldn't have thought Lorelei read the editorial section of *any* newspaper. And normally he'd be surprised that the mention of something two private citizens possibly did at a private function could be considered earth-rocking in *any* part of the world, but he'd humor her for the moment. "What did it say?"

In response, Lorelei pulled a torn page out of her purse and shoved it at him. It took a second for him to get through a rundown of the guest list, what everyone was wearing and a description of the ice sculptures, but finally he found Lorelei's name and his. He turned the paper over, looking for more, but on the back was an advertisement for a casino. "That's it?"

Lorelei's jaw dropped. "You don't think that's *enough?*"

"I don't actually see the problem, Lorelei."

She looked on the edge of a sputter. "My mother reads the Wednesday Pages like the Bible."

"As does mine. So?"

This time Lorelei did sputter. "*So?* That's all you have to say?"

"Well, I don't see a reason to freak out."

"Obviously *your* mother hasn't been texting you all morning, looking for an explanation because half the city is asking *her* for an explanation."

So *that* was what had her panties in a twist. *Damn it. I shouldn't have thought about her panties.* Especially since he knew for a fact that her taste in undergarments ran to the tiny and lacy. "Definitely not."

"Well, that figures."

He could hear the sour *that must be nice* tone under those words. "Look, Lorelei. We don't owe anyone an explanation for anything—much less some busybody's baseless speculation in what is little more than a gossip column."

Lorelei's eyes widened. "'Baseless speculations?'"

"Well, it was baseless—at least until your little freak-out gave it credence. The very fact you came running down here makes it look like there really *is* something going on. Something more than what was publicly witnessed. Someone went fishing and you took the bait. You've pretty much told the world we had sex."

Her eyes widened. "For the love of..." Lorelei obviously hadn't thought it through until now, and the realization set her pacing in frustration. She started muttering to herself, and he caught the occasional phrase about her mother or Vivi killing her. Even Connor's name came up once. Finally she stopped pacing and turned to him. "What do you suggest we do?"

He didn't see the big deal. "*We* don't do anything. *I'm* going to go about my business as always. *You* can do whatever you think best."

"Donovan, I'm asking for your help here. You may not care that there's gossip in the paper, but I do."

"Since when?" There was certain information a person couldn't avoid, no matter how uninterested they might be. That included news of the adventures of the young, wealthy, beautiful and fabulous. Lorelei had made the papers plenty of times with far more descriptive rundowns on her activities.

"I know I haven't cared in the past, but things are different now."

Her voice lost the impatience and the snark, and for a moment she sounded almost vulnerable. But she was completely overreacting. This was not nearly the catastrophe Lorelei seemed to think it was, and, left alone, it would all blow over soon enough.

"I know I've never been a saint like Vivi. Never will be, either." She smiled weakly, and he realized that it had to be tough to live up to an example like Vivi. "The thing is, with Vivi and Connor on their honeymoon, I'm going to be making appearances on their behalf—for the charities they represent and the organizations they support. I don't need—and can't have—this kind of gossip hanging over my head and coloring everyone's thoughts." Lorelei's blue eyes were wide and earnest. She was serious. "It's not just about me. It's about them and their reputations and the organizations they do so much for. There's a lot more at stake than just a little public embarrassment for me."

He normally didn't have any patience for the troubles of the children of the city's elite. Connor and Vivi had been the exceptions that had slowly brought him around to a different view. They hadn't sat on their trust funds or relied on family connections to coast through in a perfect life. They'd worked hard: Connor with his music career and Vivi with her art gallery and work with every non-profit organization in the parish. *That* he respected.

If Lorelei had hit him with anything else…

Damn. He felt himself buckling. When had he become such a sucker for a damsel in distress?

"Who did the write-up?"

Lorelei looked relieved as he relented. She glanced at the article for its byline. "Evelyn Jones."

He knew Evelyn slightly through the newspaper. Her true calling was in tabloid gossip, and the New Orleans society pages were the closest she'd gotten. "Was she a guest at the wedding?"

Lorelei seemed to be thinking. "She was *there*. I'm pretty sure she left after the cake-cutting, though."

"Then she's reporting hearsay. Everyone in the bar that night was just as far gone as we were."

"Except for the servers—"

"And the one who gave up *that* little tidbit probably got a nice fat tip for the story."

"That's a terrible—"

He shrugged off her outrage. "That's the way it works.

For a hundred bucks I could get a source to swear they once saw Mother Theresa doing keg stands. Times are tough all around. Money talks."

Lorelei looked outraged. "That's dishonest."

"That's tabloid journalism for you."

"And you wonder why—"

"I don't wonder anything, Lorelei. It is what it is."

"So *you'd* sell someone's reputation out just for money?" She looked worried. He assumed she'd only just now realized that he now had quite the story about her to sell. He wouldn't even have to lie or embellish it, either.

"Calm down. I see no need to spread the news, and I certainly don't need the money."

Lorelei shot him a look he couldn't decipher. Then she sighed and sank back onto the couch. "So how do I disprove something when I don't know how much of it is true? I'm not a very good liar." The corners of her mouth turned down as she confessed that like it was a character flaw.

"We did not engage in any PDA at the bar. It was later that…" He trailed off as Lorelei flushed that rosy color. "We laugh it off. That's it. We and the others were just having a good time—as one does at a party—and any other claims have been exaggerated for effect."

Lorelei started to nod, but caught herself. "Wait a second…" A suspicious look began to pull her eyebrows together. "How are you so certain that there was no PDA in the bar? You told me it was all fuzzy from the tequila."

Damn. She'd caught that. "Fuzzy, yes. Total blackout… no."

"So you do…remember?" The suspicion on her face turned to horror, and then that rosy embarrassed color she'd had since he'd brought up PDA deepened to an amazing shade of red. She crossed her arms over her chest again, but this time it was more a gesture of modesty, like he could see through her clothes. "Oh, my *God*. It was bad enough to know it happened even though I didn't remember it. But to know that you do and I don't…"

Now he felt like some kind of pervert, which made absolutely no sense at all. And he had no idea what he should say to take that vulnerable, disgusted-with-herself look off her face.

"Did I—? Did we…?" Lorelei pushed to her feet and picked up her purse. "Oh, God. I have to leave now."

"It was just sex, Lorelei."

"Oh, well, *that* completely alleviates my mind. Thank you."

"You want a rundown? A play-by-play?"

Her eyes widened. "You could provide that?"

He let his silence answer her question.

She swallowed hard and cleared her throat. "Oh, this just keeps getting better and better."

Now he felt like a *twisted* pervert. "Lorelei…"

She squared her shoulders. "I think you're right, Donovan. We should just ignore the innuendo and laugh it off if anyone has the bad manners to bring it up. Forgetting it ever happened doesn't seem to be an option anymore—at least for *you*—but we'll go with pretending it didn't." Lorelei grabbed her purse from the couch and a bitter laugh escaped. "I mean, who's really going to believe it, right? Me and you? Please. *I* can barely believe it. It's absurd."

The more she tried to convince herself, the more insulted he got. He wasn't a leper, for God's sake, and most women wouldn't be acting as if they'd committed some gross, shameful, unforgivable sin like Lorelei was. Most *normal* women—women who weren't like Lorelei and her ilk—considered him a pretty good catch and would be trying to capitalize on this instead of flagellating themselves over it. Their hook-up might have been insane, but it certainly hadn't crossed over into the absurd. They were both of the same species, whether Lorelei wanted to admit that or not.

She might not remember it, but she'd enjoyed herself. It wasn't as if he'd forced her into his bed, either. She'd been a willing, active participant who'd gone to sleep with a smile on her face.

His ego had had just about enough of the martyr act, and when Lorelei tried to brush past him, heading for the door, still muttering about absurdity, he grabbed her elbow and turned her to face him.

"*I* won't have the 'bad manners' to bring this up the next time we meet, Princess, but at least let me leave you with the truth. It was hot, sweaty, athletic sex, and you enjoyed it. You're quite flexible, you know."

Lorelei swallowed hard. He had to give her credit, though. She met his eyes and never wavered as he described, in graphic detail, the way she'd ridden him like a polo pony and begged for more. Her pupils dilated until only a small ring of blue remained, and her breathing turned shallow. But as his skin heated with the memory and his erection pressed painfully against his zipper, he cursed the fact he'd let his ego and pride take it this far. Being this close to Lorelei allowed the scent of her perfume to fill his nose with each breath, sending sharp pangs through his belly. Even the soft skin of her arm where he held it seemed to sear his fingers. When her tongue snaked out to moisten her lips he could practically feel it moving over his skin instead.

The air around them felt charged and heavy, and time slowed to a standstill as he let his eyes wander down to her lips and then to the pink flush climbing out of her cleavage. He had so much more to throw at her, but the words seemed trapped in his chest under the desire to do something entirely different.

Lorelei closed her eyes and took a deep but unsteady breath. When her eyes met his again he saw regret there. "You know, the worst part of this isn't what other people might think."

He braced himself.

"What really kills me is that you remember it and I don't."

The words were out there before Lorelei could stop them, and Donovan's sharp intake of breath had her regretting them instantly. The moment he'd touched her, though, every nerve in her body had cried out, wanting more of what her mind couldn't quite remember but her skin obviously did.

And his *words*... Crude as they were, they had spoken to something inside her, awakening that same feeling of frustration she'd faced every morning this week. The achy need in her core, the shivers in her belly... She wanted to find the cause and the cure.

Donovan is both, her mind whispered.

Lorelei gritted her teeth. That wasn't an option. The last thing she needed right now was to get involved with anybody. This was a time to focus on her professional life, not her personal life. Hell, it was probably that focus that had led her to Donovan's bed in the first place; she hadn't had the time for a social life—and hadn't wanted the scrutiny, either—and celibacy must not sit well with her. If she gave in to that little whisper, it could torpedo everything.

She stepped back quickly, breaking the web of heat and electricity that had snared her and led to that embarrassing admission. The air felt cooler immediately, and rationality returned. At least until she looked at Donovan. His eyes were hot, his body tense. It awoke something primal in her that was almost impossible to ignore.

She swallowed hard. Once again she needed a dignified exit. "I've got to go."

She didn't wait for a response, and focused instead on looking casual and carefree as she left Donovan's office. Donovan was right: coming here had just given that one sentence legs to stand on, so she forced herself to look unbothered. Normal.

She pasted a false smile on her face and kept her head up as she exited the building and crossed to the lot across the street where she'd parked. Once safely inside, with the doors locked and the AC running full-blast, the pride that had buoyed her out of there deflated.

Not only was she never drinking again, she was going to go online today and order herself a chastity belt. Maybe she should just drive straight to the convent and beg to be taken in for her own protection. There had to be something really disturbingly wrong in her brain for her to be in this position.

To be honest, one line in a newspaper was nothing. She'd had far more accurate and damaging reports printed about her before. Her mother's garden club might be twittering about it—but, honestly, it would pass. It wouldn't be the first time she'd downplayed something until it went away. No, she had to face the fact that she'd grabbed on to to the flimsiest of excuses to go and see Donovan and ended up having her worst suspicions confirmed.

It was one thing to have no shame; it was another thing entirely to realize she had no pride, either.

That's not true. She did have her pride. The fact she'd gotten the information she wanted and was currently sitting in her car *alone* was proof she possessed a spine *and* self-control. Her dignity might be a little dented, but her pride was intact.

If feeling a little shaky.

In a way, she should be glad that Donovan was at the center of this debacle. It wasn't as if their paths crossed often—they traveled in different circles—so she wouldn't have to face him repeatedly, knowing the whole time that he was able to picture her... *Ugh.*

Time would work its magic, and probably by the time she saw him again this would be an even fuzzier memory—and hopefully she'd be past the chemical reaction he seemed to cause.

Her mom's ringtone sounded again, and this time she answered. "I'm sorry I haven't had the chance to call you back. I've had a busy morning." That was true; panic had kept her quite busy.

"Where *are* you?"

"I'm on my way to Connor's studio." That wasn't a lie, either; the St. James Media building was sort of on her way. "I've got some work to catch up on."

"And are you going to tell me what that comment about you and Donovan St. James is about?"

Lorelei forced herself to laugh. It sounded fake and hollow to her ears, but her mother didn't seem to notice. "There was an after-party and we were both there, but... me and Donovan St. James? That's insane."

That wasn't a lie, either.

CHAPTER THREE

"But you said you'd stand in for Vivienne while she was on her honeymoon. They're expecting you to be there."

That was before I knew what I was getting myself into.

Standing in for Vivi had sounded like a good idea—it would give her a chance to show that her sister wasn't the only one with saintly, service-oriented tendencies *and* get her out there as Connor's representative—but she hadn't had a full understanding of what Vivi's life was really like when she'd hatched that plan. Oh, she knew in *theory* that Vivi was busy and involved in everything, but actually inheriting even part of that schedule had left her wondering how Vivi had time to do anything else. Like sleep. She sighed into the phone. "I know, Mom, but I think I'm getting a migraine."

"You've never had a migraine in your life."

I never had Donovan St. James turning up everywhere like a bad penny before, either.

She'd finally read the emails from Vivi about her schedule. After her shock at how dense that schedule actually was had passed, she'd nearly choked when her preparations for those events had informed her that Donovan was also all over that schedule. Somehow she'd missed the memo that outlined how he'd gotten neck-deep into the city's business. No wonder Vivi and Connor had invited him to the wedding. If nothing else, it was professional courtesy.

"Well, it's a killer headache, regardless."

"Your father and I have tickets for the ballet with the Allisons. You'll have to solider through. It will be a challenge, but—"

"LaBlancs love a challenge," Lorelei finished for her. "I know."

"You'll do fine, darling. Even with a headache."

Her mom's words brought a smile to her face even in her misery. *Finally she was getting somewhere.*

"Just be friendly and gracious. Stick to club soda and remember to think before you speak."

And there was the dig. Lord, it was hard to live down a reputation.

Eventually, though, she'd live it down. Even if it killed her in the process.

Her mother hung up and Lorelei leaned her head back against the couch. In reality she was pretty much ready to go—and early, at that—but panic had set in, causing her to call her mom for a way out of this mess.

The headache, while not as debilitating as she'd claimed, *was* real—and it was named Donovan. She thought longingly of the bottle of Chardonnay in the fridge as a solution. But even if she hadn't sworn off drinking, hadn't she already proved beyond a shadow of a doubt that she, Donovan and alcohol were a bad, bad mix?

Of course she probably shouldn't worry about Donovan's part in that cocktail. Her personal humiliation was bad enough, but Donovan had to be wondering who'd given her a day pass from the asylum. Just the thought of facing him again… And so soon after the last debacle…

Suck it up, kiddo. The third time *had* to be a charm. She was a LaBlanc, for God's sake; she needed to start acting like one. If she had to channel Vivi, or her mother, or even the Queen of England to get through this with poise and class, she would.

She knew what she had to do; she knew she could do it. Her plan was solid—even if the execution wasn't a sure thing.

Her dress hung on the closet door: a deep blue to match her eyes, with a modest but not matronly neckline, and a hem that hit just above the knee. It was age-appropriate—youthful without being trashy—and stylish without falling into the "trendy" trap.

It was also Vivi's. But she'd told herself that if she was going to do Vivi's job she needed Vivi's wardrobe. Right now it looked like a suit of armor, ready to protect her from herself.

Yes, the dress was completely appropriate, and Lorelei suddenly hated it. She might need to channel her sister, her mother and the freakin' queen to do this right, but she wasn't going to betray herself, either. She was letting Donovan have way too much control of her mind, letting him shake her already shaky confidence in herself.

She wasn't stupid, and she wasn't *that* much of a screw-up. She had the manners and the experience to get through this, but if she tried too hard to be something—or someone—she wasn't, everyone would know she was faking it.

And she didn't want to fake it. She didn't *need* to fake it. She could do so much more than anyone assumed; she just needed the chance to show them that. She wanted to be accepted on her own terms and for her own merits—not just because she was a LaBlanc. She had an uphill climb, though. She'd broken or flaunted every rule and edict ever laid down, and the old guard was not exactly forgiving. She couldn't just reclaim her birthright—she was going to have to earn it back.

But she could. She just needed to find that happy medium.

And it started with a different dress.

Donovan had never quite outgrown the sick kick he got out of attending events like this.

As much as they might try to deny it publicly, New Orleans society was an old, established hierarchy, and it galled many members of that hierarchy to open its ranks even the tiniest bit. But Old Money wasn't quite what it had used to be so, like it or not, those ranks had had to make exceptions. Even for a family like his that many still considered to be only a step above carpetbaggers. Oh, they had to respect his money, and his money bought influence—even if they didn't like it one little bit.

The truth was—and it had taken him a while to figure it out— that the Old Guard were scared of that influence, scared they were losing their monopoly to upstarts and the trashy nouveau riche. If anything, they were closing the ranks even tighter and drawing very clear lines in the sand.

For him, though, it was more than just his New Money and lower-class roots that they disliked. With him, it was personal. He'd brought down some of their own. He was a social pariah—but not one who could be ignored. And they didn't like that at all.

He'd admit he still got a bit of immature glee sometimes over the situation, but the reality was that he really did support the mission of the Children's Music Project and was more than happy to sit on the board. "Nouveau riche" might not be a title he'd shake anytime soon, but he and his nouveau riche friends were the prime check-

writers these days. Times really were tough all around—
especially for those who'd lost a bundle in the market
crash. Genteel poverty in the upper classes was a New Orleans tradition that dated back to Reconstruction—which
only underscored the fact that the right DNA was more
important than a healthy bank balance, and the lack of
that DNA would forever keep certain doors locked tight.

He went to the bar to refill his drink as the CMP's
executive director took to the small stage that normally
contained the house band. There were general thanks, a
rundown of the year's successes, plans for the future…

Jack Morgan, a partner in the law firm that represented
St. James Media and an occasional racketball partner when
no one else was available, joined him at the bar and signaled for a refill, as well. "How long do you think the
speeches will last?"

"Why? Got a hot date?"

"Would that get me out of here?" Jack slid a bill across
the bar and then rested against it with a sigh.

"Make a run for it. No one will notice you're gone."

"My mother will."

Donovan snorted. Mrs. Morgan was a true dragon of
the old order. "Sucks to be you."

"Tonight it does."

"…Lorelei LaBlanc," the director announced.

That got his attention, snapping his head toward the
stage so fast his neck cramped. His first thought—*What
the hell is Lorelei doing here?*—was rebutted by remembering the remark she'd made Wednesday about stepping
in for Vivi and Connor while they were on their honeymoon. Still…he'd seen her more in the last week than he
had in the last five years.

Then Lorelei emerged from the crowd to climb the

steps to the stage, and he nearly dropped the drink he held in his hand.

Wrapped in a curve-hugging deep purple dress, she looked like a princess addressing the motley masses. Lorelei was the epitome of elegance, style and class, a product of extremely good breeding. She wore it easily, confidently. That black hair curled around creamy shoulders and tendrils snaked over her breast like a caress. Want streaked through him like a flash, and the low whistle he heard from beside him proved he wasn't the only one feeling it.

"Damn," Jack muttered. "Little sis grew up nicely."

He considered Jack more of an acquaintance than a friend, so it was tough to allow him to keep his teeth as the compliments continued.

Lorelei's smile was blinding as she took the microphone from the director. "Vivienne hasn't missed one of these events in years, and she didn't want to miss this one, either, but she hopes you'll forgive her since it's her honeymoon." Lorelei paused as polite applause moved through the crowd. "And before you ask…yes, I do know where they are. But, no, I won't tell you where they went. You'll just have trust me when I tell you it's fabulous and they're having a wonderful time."

A laugh rippled through the crowd. He had to admit Lorelei knew how to command a crowd's attention.

"I'm not just here tonight on behalf of my sister. I'm here for Connor and ConMan Studios, as well."

At the mention of Connor's name the low rumble of conversation in the crowd died instantly.

"As you can imagine, music and music education is a cause very close to Connor's heart. CMP has focused, by necessity, on in-school programs for younger children…"

Lorelei looked comfortable up there, and if public

speaking was one of her fears it certainly didn't show in her speech or body language. She had that same presence that Donovan had seen in her sister—that confidence that could only come from the security of knowing exactly who she was. Unlike her sister, though, Lorelei had a low, hypnotic timbre in her voice that sounded like pure sex to him.

It did bad things to his equilibrium.

"It's my great privilege to announce tonight that Con-Man Studios is partnering with the CMP to expand its summer programs for the area's youth by providing not only funding, but space and access to some of the city's best musical talent." She paused for the applause, and then said with a laugh, "We have big plans in the works, so rest assured you'll all be hearing from me very soon. And often."

There was shock that Lorelei was going to be so involved with whatever plans Connor had cooked up with Vivi for his project, but it didn't cancel out the slice of desire that cut him at the sound of that husky laugh.

In broad strokes Lorelei outlined the basics of the plan, preparing folks to open their checkbooks. It took a moment for him to realize she kept saying "me" and "I." She'd started this speech as a Vivi substitute, but it was now becoming clear that Lorelei would be playing an active role. *That* was new. Lorelei hadn't had much involvement with anything beyond the periphery until now. And she seemed genuinely excited about it, as well. The universe was slightly askew.

To more applause, Lorelei handed back the microphone and left the stage, quickly being swallowed into the crowd.

Jack let out another low whistle, jerking Donovan's attention back since he'd long since forgotten Jack was even standing there. "I never had a thing for either of the

LaBlanc girls back in high school, but I'm rethinking that now." He pushed away from the bar and patted Donovan on the shoulder. "See ya."

"Where are you going?"

Jack grinned. "To gather my thoughts, of course."

There was that need to punch Jack again. It made no sense whatsoever, but he was starting to get used to the feeling.

Why do I care?

"Well, hello there."

He turned and found Jessica Reynald flashing a broad smile and ample cleavage. He did not need this now. After listening to Lorelei's straight-sex voice he was primed— but not for Jess Reynald. He'd been caught by her smile and her cleavage in a brief moment of insanity six months ago, and it had been nothing short of disastrous. Jess's family had made their money in commercial properties, and they'd initially bonded over their similar still-not-good-enough circumstances. But Jess was desperate to eventually break into those circles that excluded her, and that desperation to be accepted had turned him off. Jess, though, wasn't one to give up. She was looking to marry into the upper class—he wondered how long it would be before she realized that just wasn't going to happen—but until then she was willing to make do with him.

"I was hoping to find you here, Donovan. It's been a long time."

Now the universe is just screwing with me. "Not really. Only a couple of months."

"Where've you been hiding?"

"In plain sight. I've been really busy."

"But all work and no play is not good," she purred as she stepped closer. The heavy rose scent of her perfume nearly choked him. "I heard there's a great new jazz club that just opened over off Tchoupitoulas Street at Poydras. This is getting boring. Why don't we go check it out?"

"Not tonight, Jess."

She pouted and moved even closer, letting her breasts rest heavily on his arm. After his salivating over Lorelei's elegance and class, Jessica seemed overblown. "So when, then? I've missed you."

He heard a snort—quickly covered by a cough—and when he looked up he saw Jack and Lorelei at the bar, close enough to have heard Jess's purr and invitation. That snort had come from her.

"Well, Donovan?" Jess rose up on to her tiptoes, her lips only inches from his ear. "Haven't you missed me even a little bit?"

Lorelei rolled her eyes before turning back to Jack with a smile and letting him lead her away.

Damn it.

Lorelei smiled at the doorman as he opened the door and offered to call for a taxi, but the smile felt stiff on her face. She'd done nothing but smile all night, whether she wanted to or not. Her cheeks might never recover.

She *should* be happy, she reminded herself. She'd done well in there, and though she'd officially been standing in for Vivi and Connor, she'd talked to enough people to get the word spreading that she was stepping up to the plate in her own right, as well. She had several commitments of support for next summer's workshops, and when Connor got back they'd have lots to follow up on. She'd seen and been seen, shaken all the right hands, and she hadn't done anything that would even raise an eyebrow.

And Jack Morgan, who'd never so much as given her the time of day in high school—or since, for that matter—

had spent the last forty-five minutes flirting with her. In front of his mother, no less.

Tonight could be chalked up as a success all the way around. She'd done it. She'd pat herself on the back if she could, but that headache named Donovan had only gotten worse. A couple of people had mentioned the comment in the paper to her, but she'd laughed it off—and the people who'd mentioned it were exactly the kind who'd spread anything remotely gossiplike, so hopefully her response would shut down any other speculation.

The cause of her headache had ignored her all evening. That fact hadn't really bothered her—much—until she'd seen Jessica Reynald resting her impressive bosom on Donovan's arm and making cow's eyes at him. And Donovan hadn't exactly been fighting her off. The man was nothing more than a hound dog. And if last Saturday night hadn't felt cheap and tawdry enough, that just pushed it right over the edge into sordid.

It's none of my business who he sleeps with. I'm just another notch in his bedpost. It was downright embarrassing.

"Leaving already?"

She spun so fast at the sound of the last voice on earth she wanted to hear right then that her heel caught in a sidewalk crack, causing her to wobble dangerously. Quickly righting herself, she snapped, "Are you *following* me now?"

Donovan stepped back. "Whoa, you've got one hell of an ego there, Princess."

There was something so snide in the way he called her Princess that it put her teeth on edge. "Why *are* you here?"

A look of complete confused innocence crossed his face. "Because I'm leaving and this is the way out."

The reasonableness of the statement left her feeling a

bit silly. That feeling caused her to snark, "Alone? What happened to Jessica?"

"I could ask you what happened to Jack."

"That's absolutely none of your business."

An eyebrow went up. "But Jess is yours?"

Damn it. She squared he shoulders and looked around, determined to limit their conversation since ignoring him was going to be difficult. "Why are there no taxis?"

"To annoy you, I'm sure."

The doorman returned, thankfully forestalling the comeback she desperately wanted to make but shouldn't. "Dispatch says it's going to be about twenty minutes. Lot of things letting out right now."

She tried to keep the frustration out of her voice. This wasn't his fault. "Thank you."

"Why don't you ask Jack to give you a ride home?"

There was an edge to Donovan's voice that she didn't like. "You know, I'm actually thinking a short walk might be nice."

"Do you have a death wish?"

"How patronising of you. I'm an adult, and more than capable of taking care of myself. It's not even ten o'clock, and it's a populated area. I'll be perfectly safe."

"I meant your shoes. You'll kill yourself in those things."

"They're quite comfortable." That wasn't exactly a lie. They *were* quite comfortable—provided she was indoors and able to sit occasionally. An eight-block hike down Esplanade was a different situation entirely. That was why she'd asked for a cab in the first place. "I'll be fine. Good night, Donovan."

Proud of herself, she began the trek home. This would be good for her, she told herself. It would give her a chance to clear her mind, enjoy the sights. This part of Esplanade was heavily residential—folks out with their dogs, tourists exploring… It would be nice. And good exercise.

Within seconds, though, she began to rethink the idea: the temperature had dropped to a reasonable degree, but the humidity was still high and her skin felt damp already. She'd barely gone a block before her heel caught in another crack and nearly sent her sprawling.

She groaned as she righted herself. Pride and stubbornness would be her downfall one day.

Donovan's laugh floated down the street to her ears. "That was graceful."

Don't take the bait, her brain warned, but she was already turning around. "And you're obnoxious and immature." She held on to a streetlight and wiggled her ankle experimentally.

Note to self: Buy some of those little foldable flats and keep them in your purse.

Better note to self: Next time ignore him and wait for a cab.

Even better note to self: Don't let there be a next time. Avoid him at all costs.

She looked up from her mental lecture to see Donovan closing in. "Are you all right?"

So much for 'no next time.' Or maybe she could consider this the same time as earlier. "I'm fine."

"I was just being polite, Princess—making sure you hadn't hurt yourself."

"That's very kind of you. However…" *time to be brutally honest* "…in case you haven't noticed, I'm trying very hard to ignore you."

"I thought we were pretending it never happened?"

"We are."

"Then why the need to ignore me?"

God, why was he being so difficult? "Because it would

be much easier for me to actually do the pretending if you weren't around."

"You're overreacting. We're adults. It was consensual—if not intentional. It's not half as big a deal as you're making it out to be."

A man walking his dog slowed his steps as he passed, the look on his face a mixture of concern and interest. Lorelei bit back the words on the tip of her tongue. Reaching for Donovan's arm, she dragged him a few feet away from the street into the shadows. "Believe it or not, I'm not in the habit of sleeping with random men. I find this situation to be awkward and quite disturbing."

"Which part?"

That was not at all the response she'd expected, and when coupled with the fact that his voice lacked any mockery at all... She looked up and froze. Donovan was mostly in shadow, but his stance was relaxed, hands in his pockets. What she could see of his face looked genuine, with no trace of the usual smirk.

It took another second for her to register that she'd pulled him into a secluded spot—one that might be considered romantic due to the lush greenery that draped over the courtyard wall, creating a mini-bower. Donovan's white shirt stood out in the partial gloom, and he'd opened the top few buttons against the heat. He was so tall and broad-chested that even in her stilettos she was at eye-level with the hollow of his throat. The humidity had created a fine sheen of moisture across his skin, releasing the scent of his aftershave to mix with the fragrance of the hibiscus. The sounds of the Quarter were muffled, and the houses around them quiet. It felt...intimate—sultry, even—and it threw her off her game.

She swallowed hard, completely forgetting what she'd

planned to say—or even what he'd asked. "I'm sorry—what?"

"The situation is awkward and disturbing. I asked which part."

Was it her imagination, or was Donovan's voice lower and huskier than normal? The embers that had smoldered in her belly for nearly a week flared to life, the sounds and the scents around her kindling a feeling that her body remembered even if her mind didn't.

And she wanted to know.

Don't make this even worse.

But her legs felt wobbly and weak, and her hand was already reaching for him. She was setting herself up for disaster, but the draw was almost too painful to fight. Her hand landed on his chest, and she could feel the rapid beat of his heart under her palm and the jump of the muscle under the skin. Donovan wasn't immune to her, and that knowledge gave her the courage to meet his eyes. What she saw there nearly took her breath away, and the heat that flooded her had nothing to do with the weather.

"Lorelei…"

It was now or never. If she walked away now she'd regret it. But this was a huge risk; if Donovan turned her down, her humiliation would be everlasting.

Rising up on her toes until only inches separated them, she dug deep and let the ache inside her force the words out. "I want to know."

She felt the shock ripple through his body as she closed the space and let her lips meet his.

There was a pause, then everything exploded.

The sensations hit her with the force of a hurricane, cancelling out her higher brain functions. The feel and taste of Donovan was both new and familiar at the same time, giving reality to what had only been a vague craving before.

His mouth was hot and demanding, each stroke of his tongue licking her like fire and sending the sensation searing through her entire body. The solid bulk of his chest pressed against hers, anchoring her to the brick wall at her back and trapping her in a cage of warm male flesh.

It was divine.

She felt a tug on her hair and let her head fall back, allowing Donovan to press hot kisses down her neck to the sensitive skin at her collarbone. She arched against him, getting contact from breast to knee, and his hands wrapped around her waist to hold her there.

This was what she'd been trying to remember. *This* was what her body knew, what her skin had been trying to tell her about. Memories of the sensations butted at her brain, allowing her to savor the anticipation of the next touch, the next taste, while somehow knowing how good it would be at the same time.

Her fingers tightened in his hair, dragging his mouth back to hers. She melted under the onslaught.

"Lorelei…"

The sound of her name, whispered huskily next to her ear, sent goose bumps over her skin, but she heard the reluctant *this isn't a good idea* echoing underneath.

"I know." She could force herself *not* to think about all the reasons why this was a really bad idea, but they were still on a public street, only a block from the restaurant, and the shadows and the hibiscus blooms were far from the adequate privacy needed. She pressed a kiss against his neck, tasted the salt and felt the thrumming of his pulse under her lips. "I just don't—" The words were stopped as she gave in to the urge for another taste. She tightened her fingers around the collar of his jacket, unwilling to let this moment, this feeling go. "My house is seven blocks from here."

She felt Donovan smile against her temple as his hands splayed across the small of her back to pull her even closer. "Mine's four."

Her decision had been made the moment she touched him, but when he didn't move, she realized Donovan must be waiting for a response. "Sounds good."

The feel of Lorelei pressed against him was mind-scrambling, and the orders from his brain to his feet seemed to be getting lost.

Rationally, he knew this shouldn't be happening, but somehow it felt inevitable, as well. He hadn't followed her with this intent, but now he didn't know why he hadn't.

The four blocks to his house seemed ridiculously far when his body was screaming for him to take her right here, right now.

Move.

He reached for her hand and twined his fingers through hers. He realized Lorelei's hand was shaking. She wore a dazed look, her lips swollen and moist, and her breath was uneven and shallow. The woman was lust incarnate, and pure want cut deep into his belly.

Lorelei trailed slightly behind as he led her quickly across Esplanade and down Dauphine into the Quarter. When he felt resistance in her arm, he glanced over his shoulder to see Lorelei's gaze firmly on her feet and wondered if she was having second thoughts. Belatedly he realized it was those impossibly sexy shoes. The ancient and uneven sidewalks of the Quarter were treacherous, and he was practically dragging her like a caveman back to his den.

He shortened his stride and slowed his steps. Lorelei squeezed his hand in thanks without looking up.

Dauphine Street was primarily residential, and the few people out on the street didn't give them a second glance—even though Donovan felt like his erection was leading the way and their intent was obvious.

One block up St. Phillip to Burgundy and the redbrick of his house appeared like a lighthouse. The knowledge they were that close sent blood rushing to his groin so fast he had difficulty finding his keys and remembering how to make them work.

A rush of air-conditioning cooled the sweat on his skin as he pulled Lorelei inside and slammed the door behind her. The light from the hall showed a faint glistening of sweat around Lorelei's hairline and a pink flush to her cheeks that could either be from exertion or arousal.

Arousal, he decided, as Lorelei threw herself into his arms again with a force that nearly knocked him off his feet. Her arms twined around his neck, pulling his mouth to hers. In response he picked her up and headed for the stairs.

Lorelei's fingers worked on the buttons of his shirt and a hand slipped inside. The tease of her fingers over his nipple nearly caused him to miss a step. He sucked in his breath, trying to focus on remembering where his bedroom was.

Finally. It took every ounce of control he had not to fling her onto the bed and bury himself in her. Instead he set her carefully on her feet. She'd kicked off her shoes somewhere along the way, and now the top of Lorelei's head was even with his chest. She opened his shirt farther and placed a kiss on the bare skin.

He'd thought the burning, clawing need he remembered had been a byproduct of too much tequila and a trick of his mind, but as it swept through him in a fierce wave, he realized the memory was dull in comparison with the reality. Lorelei was as hypnotic and drugging as her namesake—and probably just as dangerous.

Her hands were busy, untucking his shirt and pushing it and his jacket off. Then, with an appreciative sigh, she ran her fingers from his collarbones to his belt buckle. She looked up and gave him a small smile, before turning around and lifting her hair over her shoulder to expose the zipper down the back of her dress. A second later the purple silk was in a puddle at her feet, and she was facing him wearing only a scrap of black lace.

Dear God, she was even more beautiful than he remembered. He hadn't realized he'd voiced the thought until Lorelei placed a hand on his chest and said, "I'm glad there's still some element of surprise for you."

How they got to the bed he didn't quite know, but a second later Lorelei was flat on her back, that jet-black hair tangling around her face, and he was on top of her, savoring the feel of her skin against his.

Oh, mercy, Lorelei thought. This was... It... This was... *Mercy.* She just couldn't grab hold of a thought for very long.

Donovan had amazingly soft skin draped over hard muscle, and the crisp hair on his chest left her nipples tingling. His hips moved tantalizingly as his lips mapped her skin, and she wasn't sure if she was melting or going up in flames. Hands shaking with desire, she fumbled with his belt until Donovan finally took over.

Then it was just hot skin and hands that seemed to know exactly where to touch, driving her insane and right to the very edge. Donovan's mouth... *Oh, dear God, his mouth...* She arched against him, her hands searching for purchase on the sheets as she realized the cries she heard were coming from her.

And then the wave she was on broke, her mind going blank as violent tremors shook her to her bones. She heard Donovan's growl as his mouth found hers, and he ate the scream that came when he drove into her in one hot, thrilling thrust.

Her orgasm just went on and on, and she anchored herself to Donovan's heaving torso as she rode out the waves of pleasure until she saw fireworks and the world went black.

CHAPTER FOUR

LORELEI'S EYES WERE CLOSED, but she wasn't sleeping. Even if he hadn't slept next to her before he'd know; her breath didn't have that deep, even quality of sleep. The cool sophisticate she'd been hours ago was gone. There were dark smudges under her eyes and a slight stubble burn around her mouth and jaw. That jet-black hair ran riot around her shoulders, the tangles sticking to her damp skin.

She looked earthy and sensual and far too tempting to be real.

But she was also uncharacteristically silent. Lorelei was not the quiet type, and while he really didn't care for idle pillow talk, the fact she wasn't saying anything at all bordered on unnerving. Lorelei *always* had something to say. About everything. But not right now. She faced him, but from her side of the king-size bed, leaving plenty of distance between them. So while there wasn't exactly a wall running down the middle of his bed, there was a very respectable fence.

And it was probably electrified.

That realization kept his hands to himself when they itched to reach for her again. Instead, Donovan stacked his hands behind his head and stared at the ceiling. In reality, the only thing more insane than hooking up with Lorelei was hooking up with her twice. He'd known it, but he'd let his little head do all the thinking.

What was it about Lorelei that turned him into a teenage boy who'd never laid hands on a real woman before? The lack of self-control or higher brain function was just embarrassing even to think about. Wouldn't *that* be a surprise to all those people who liked to write those "Most Eligible" articles that painted him as some sort of Creole Casanova?

"Something funny?" Lorelei's voice was husky—probably a side effect of all that screaming—and he turned toward her to see that her eyes were open and watching him. "You've got a little smile on your face."

"Why? Are you thinking you're the one who put it there?"

Her lips twitched. "If it were anyone other than you… maybe."

"*Now* who's wearing a smile?"

"Oh, I don't doubt it. *That* was pretty damn amazing."

The honesty of that purred statement floored him—figuratively speaking, at least. He was glad he was already lying down. Then Lorelei stretched, catlike, her back arching off the bed and drawing his eyes to her small but perfectly shaped breasts. The sensual movement caused his brain to short-circuit. Her skin seemed luminescent in the half light, the curves begging to be traced again. He knew how that skin felt under his hands, and how it would respond to his touch.

She laughed quietly. "I feel like I should thank you."

That got his attention. He looked at her and grinned. "Well, you're quite welcome," he answered formally.

She shot him an exasperated look, but there was humor behind it, not irritation. "I *meant* for appeasing my curiosity."

"And is it appeased?"

Lorelei stretched again—probably just to torture him—before collapsing back on to the bed with a sigh. "Definitely appeased." She grinned and rolled to her side, propping her head on her fist. "I knew it was a pity I couldn't remember last time. High marks across the board, by the way."

This was a different Lorelei. Relaxed. Not biting his head off. *How novel.* "Oh, good. I was worried."

She snorted. "Somehow I doubt that."

"And somehow I'm not surprised that you do."

The sheet across her legs shifted as she wiggled her legs. "As soon as I get full feeling back in my legs I'll get dressed and call a cab."

The casual statement did something bad to him that he couldn't quite name. Trying to keep it out of his voice, he tried for a lecherous smile. "So soon?"

"I think it's probably a wise idea." She bit her bottom lip as she looked at the sheets tangled around her. "And I'm due for one, don't you think?"

A second taste of Lorelei had only whetted his appetite for more. There were several inches of her skin he had yet to explore and, no matter how insane it was, he very much wanted Lorelei to stay exactly where she was.

Well, not *exactly* where she was; she needed to move about two feet closer. Or all the way back on top of him. That would be good.

Good Lord, when had he completely lost the big brain/little brain battle? Lorelei was offering him an easy out of this situation; he should be jumping on it, helping her into her dress and straight into a cab. Hell, he hadn't brought a woman back to his place in years for the very reason that he didn't know how to get them to leave. It was much easier to claim an early meeting or an important deadline and make a graceful exit while everyone still had a smile on their faces.

It seemed that getting Lorelei to leave wasn't going to be a problem, though. She was already pushing herself up and swinging her legs off the bed. Her movements seemed a little stiff, though, and her smile had lost its humor, becoming more forced. The casualness from just a few minutes earlier seemed to evaporate.

She reached for her dress, avoiding eye contact. "I've got to get up really early in the morning—for a breakfast meeting—so I should probably get on home."

The irony slammed into him, causing him to laugh and earning him a questioning look from Lorelei. "I never knew until right now how utterly lame that excuse actually sounds."

Shock crossed her face, but then her lips twisted in amusement. She knew she was busted, but he had to give her points for not denying it.

Lorelei stepped into her dress and began struggling with her zipper, twisting herself like a contortionist and making his shoulder hurt just watching her. Walking up behind her, he moved her hands away and they fell to her sides. She stilled, and he felt her sway slightly toward him before she straightened.

He wanted to slide his hands inside the dress, around the indentation of her waist, but he settled for just resting them on the flare of her hips, letting his thumbs stroke lightly over the bare skin of her lower back. He felt the small tremor that ran over her skin and heard her breath catch.

Neither of them moved, but the pull was real, palpable, like an iron filing trying to resist a magnet, and the small space between their bodies vibrated from it.

Zip the dress. Call her a cab.

But why?

The *why* caught him off-guard. Why should he bustle her out the door like she was some kind of bad bar hookup? He'd been working under the assumption that this was insane. Crazy. A bad idea.

But now he couldn't quite articulate why.

They weren't kids anymore; all that foolishness had to have a statute of limitations that had long since passed. Lorelei was smart, articulate, challenging—not to mention absolutely gorgeous. So why, then, was this such an insane idea? He didn't want to marry her; he just wanted to get her back to bed. Why couldn't they just enjoy this?

No reasons came immediately to mind.

What *did* come to mind was the sincere wish that she'd lean back just an inch or two... "At least let me offer you a drink or something."

"The time to buy me a drink is *before* we..." She glanced at the bed, giving him a view of her profile, and swallowed hard. "Well, it's not really necessary now."

"Lorelei—"

"Look, Donovan—" She turned as she spoke, stepping back another foot and snapping that electric strand between them. "Sorry. Go ahead."

"No, ladies first."

She ran her fingers through her hair, taming the tangles and pushing it back from her face. "I don't want you to think that this... I mean, that *I'm*..." She sighed and cursed softly. "And here I didn't think anything could be more awkward than last Sunday morning."

"Just spit it out, then."

"I just don't want *you* to think that *I* think that this— that—was...um...*anything*."

His surprise must have shown on his face, because Lorelei hurried on.

"It was great—really great—I just don't...*expect* anything from you, okay? It just...*was*. It's not—well, it's not... Well, you know?"

Lorelei couldn't keep eye contact, and Donovan found his temper rising as she muddled through her speech. "No, I don't know. I'm not sure that was even English."

She sighed. "I'm just trying to say that it's all good now. I don't expect this to be anything other than what it was. Or that it's supposed to become anything."

"I have to give you credit for honesty."

Her smile was weak. "Thanks."

"But that doesn't make what you're saying sound any less insulting and tawdry."

She shook her head. "Oh, don't be so thin-skinned. It's not tawdry, and there's no need to take it personally. I'm just trying to move past this."

"Dare I ask why?"

"Because I think it's pretty clear that's the best idea. For both of us." She shrugged. "It's not like this can go anywhere."

"I don't recall saying I wanted it to."

"Then what's the problem?"

That was an excellent question. He only wished he had an answer for it. He leaned against the foot of the bed. "Not quite a week ago you told me to forget it ever happened, yet here you are."

Lorelei's mouth twisted. "I know."

"Am I supposed to believe that this time you really, *really* mean it?"

"That would be nice." She sighed, but then caught herself and crossed her arms over her chest. "You were pretty adamant about the whole forget-it-happened-thing yourself, yet here we are again."

"Hey, *you* kissed *me*."

"You weren't exactly fighting me off," she fired back.

There was that. "I'm only human, Lorelei."

"As am I." She sighed. "I'll be honest with you. You're a good-looking guy, and there's obviously chemistry between us. But we're adults, and it looks like we're going to be running into each other now. These chemistry experiments have to stop."

"Because God forbid two healthy, consenting adults have sex just because they want to?"

He watched her swallow and then lift her chin. "Something like that."

Whatever. Lorelei should carry a warning label because, as a whole, she could drive a man right off the edge. And since he valued his sanity, he should probably just let this go. She had a point about chemistry: it was a great thing, but it could also be very dangerous and blow up in your face.

So why were they both still standing here?

"Then go."

Donovan's words dropped like a gauntlet and Lorelei felt like a fool. An idiot. The right thing to do would be to breeze right out of here, head held high.

But her feet felt nailed to the floor.

It didn't help that Donovan was stark naked—and seemingly completely unselfconscious about it—and the evidence of what she'd be walking away from was impossible to ignore. She tried keeping her eyes on his face, but he looked like a freakin' sex god, all tousled and sexy, and her mouth watered at the *acres* of skin and muscle to be explored and appreciated. And even though he was basically telling her to get lost, it was also *very* clear that he was interested in something else entirely…

Donovan cleared his throat and she snapped her eyes up, finding a focus spot on the wall above the headboard.

"If you're going—go. Just lock the door behind you."

Really, the only thing this lacked was him tossing cab fare at her. She didn't know she could feel humiliated and irate at the same time. "There's no need to be a complete ass about it."

"You got what you wanted. Your curiosity has been appeased. And you don't want to be too tired for that breakfast meeting."

Donovan sounded downright annoyed about the whole thing. Which, coming from someone like him, seemed implausible enough to be amusing. The idea that she might have *offended* him was just…well, impossible.

Now she was standing here in Donovan's bedroom, barefoot, her dress gaping at the front because it still wasn't zipped, with a naked and *damn* pretty man who a few minutes ago had asked her to stay practically throwing her out onto the street while her legs were still wobbly from the most mind-blowing orgasm of her entire life. And she was ready to leave—*should* leave—but she didn't really want to now.

Her life had turned into a farce. An X-rated farce.

Make a decision. Any decision. Do something other than just stand here. Leaving was obviously the best option, but she hesitated. Why *shouldn't* she take what he was offering? There were no strings attached: just a chance to relax and burn some sexual energy without anything being messy and complicated later. It seemed so simple, so easy…and so tempting.

She took a deep breath. "Actually, I'm kind of thirsty."

Both of Donovan's eyebrows went up.

"I'll, um, call and reschedule that meeting."

When Donovan didn't move Lorelei wanted to die.

She'd read the whole thing wrong. He'd been messing with her. She should have pried her feet off the floor, not gotten pulled into a conversation. Now she'd have to kill him.

Then Donovan held out a hand. Relief rushed through her—only to be quickly swamped by a wave of desire once she touched him and his fingers curled around hers. He pulled her the few steps toward him until she stood between his thighs. Without breaking eye contact, he moved his hands to the straps of her dress, sliding them down her arms until the dress puddled on the floor again.

His hands splayed over her hips, sliding down over the outside of her thighs, then up to her waist. Strong fingers traced her ribs, then her breasts and her collarbones. Hooded eyes followed the path of his hands in an inspection that should have left her blushing and feeling exposed, but left her sizzling silently instead. She felt powerful, sexy, worshiped.

When Donovan began to retrace his path with his lips, her muscles began to melt. She swayed and reached for his shoulders for support. When his tongue slipped into her navel, her knees buckled, and only his hands on her hips kept her on her feet.

Mercy.

Curiosity killed the cat.

But the cat would die happy.

A loud, embarrassing growl from her stomach had Donovan tossing her a Saints jersey that hung nearly to her knees and leading her down to the kitchen a couple of hours later. He produced a bottle of wine and poured her a large glass. "A drink. As promised."

She laughed. "Finally."

"Now for food…" Donovan opened the fridge door and stared inside.

Donovan's house had barely registered in her brain when she'd arrived, but now she couldn't help but notice. The bedroom had been gorgeous—sumptuous and relaxing, without being overdone or competing with the view from the balcony doors—and that sumptuous, tasteful feel extended through the rest of the house. The interior renovations were very modern, with clean lines and a masculine décor that complemented the exposed brick walls and high ceilings of the original architecture. So many people renovated the charm and personality out of these older homes, and it pleased her to see that wasn't the case here.

"Your house is gorgeous. Did you do the renovations?"

He looked over his shoulder at her and grinned. "Not personally."

"But you approved the design?"

"Yep. Feel free to look around while I get us something to eat."

Honestly, watching Donovan prepare food wearing nothing but a pair of jeans had more appeal. *Mercy,* she could happily stare at him all night long, but staring *was* a little rude. She picked up her glass and wandered into the living room.

The fireplace and mantel looked to be original to the house, but it was the attention to detail that impressed her. Either Donovan or his designer had an excellent eye and a love for the historic bones of the house.

There was the requisite enormous television stationed across from a leather recliner that looked buttery soft, and a wall full of CDs and DVDs. A quick glance at the alphabetized titles told her that Donovan was both very organized and extremely eclectic in his tastes. There was a bit of everything from jazz to punk and *Casablanca* to *Shaun of the Dead.*

French doors led from that room to a courtyard behind

the house. She opened the door and stepped outside onto the patio, where the bricks still radiated warmth captured from the summer sun. Lights flipped on at her movement and she caught her breath.

High walls and lush plants provided privacy and created a feeling of seclusion in the middle of one of the busiest neighborhoods on earth. Iron benches provided seating to her right, and to her left was what looked like a large round pond. On closer inspection it proved to be a whirlpool. Dipping in a toe, she noticed it was cool water, not hot, just perfect for warm, muggy summer nights. Lorelei sat, letting her feet dangle into the pool as she listened to the night sounds.

The house, the garden—both were beautiful. But not at all the kind of place she'd thought Donovan would live. He seemed more like a high-rise condo or urban loft type of person: all brushed nickel and glass and—

She stopped the thought. *Why* had she assumed that? And when had she come to that conclusion, for that matter? She barely knew him—at least not in a way that would have given her insights into his natural habitat.

It was shocking and a little disconcerting how little she actually knew about him—beyond his award-worthy skills in that decadent bed upstairs. What did *that* say about her?

"There you are. Aren't you hot out here?"

Donovan was coming out of the house, juggling a tray with the bottle of wine tucked under his arm and the other wineglass held upside down by the stem.

"I like being outside on summer nights—even if it is muggy. There's just something real and grounding about a warm night…" She trailed off at his amusement. "I just like it. But if you don't, we can go back inside."

"No. It's why I have a garden." He put down the tray

and sat cross-legged next to her on the apron of the pool. "As promised—food."

Lorelei eyeballed the tray and stifled a laugh. Baby carrots and dip, a bag of potato chips, and a heaping plate of pizza rolls. She didn't know what she'd expected him to produce, but it hadn't been this. "You eat like a college student."

"No, I *cook* like a college student. That's why I normally eat out."

"I haven't had pizza rolls in years. They're so bad for you."

"So many of the best things in life are."

She wondered if she should include Donovan in that list. Or if he was including her in his.

Shaking the thought away, she reached for one. They were hot, fresh from the microwave, with cheese and sauce oozing out of the seams. She popped it into her mouth and closed her eyes as she chewed. Over-processed, fat-laden, high-sodium bliss exploded over her tongue. She groaned quietly as she savored it. When she opened her eyes, Donovan was staring at her, his glass halfway to his mouth.

He cleared his throat and shifted slightly. "Damn, they must be good. That's the face you make when—"

She frowned at him and he stopped. Nodding thanks at his belated discretion, she sipped at her wine. Chasing a pizza roll with a glass of excellent wine—and very expensive, based on the label—was almost surreal. But it fit with the situation somehow.

Tonight, as a whole, seemed outside the bounds of reality. The fund-raiser seemed like ancient history. Even taking the stage on Vivi and Connor's behalf no longer seemed like a monumental achievement etched in time. Time, for all intents and purposes, had stopped. It was very late—or possibly very early; she had no idea—she'd had a long, stressful day and a longer evening of downright gymnastic sex that would test anyone's stamina. She should be exhausted.

But she wasn't. And she was having a good time. It didn't bear close scrutiny, but she was, nonetheless.

They ate in silence for a while, but it wasn't an uncomfortable one.

"I meant to tell you that you did a good job tonight. At the fund-raiser," he clarified.

The compliment wasn't the most effusive ever, but coming from Donovan it seemed like very high praise. "Thanks."

"You're a natural when it comes to working a crowd." *Wow. Really high praise.*

"How much money did you get commitments for?"

"Some," she hedged, "but not as much as I'd like. How much can I put *you* down for?"

Donovan laughed. "See—a natural."

"Thank you." She gave him a regal nod. "But I'd still like a firm commitment on a dollar amount. I'm constantly amazed at how cheap rich people can be. The population of that room tonight probably has over half the wealth of the entire city, but you'd think I was taking food straight out of their children's mouths."

Donovan laughed. "Very true."

Too late she realized she'd opened a door, and braced herself for Donovan to come back with one of his scathing remarks about "elites" and "class." But he didn't go there. Instead he reached for one of the pizza rolls.

"I'm sure Jack will write you a fat check, though. He seemed keen on impressing you."

If anyone other than Donovan had said that she'd think that odd tone was jealousy. "Here's a newsflash: Jack Morgan will pinch a nickel until the buffalo burps. He promised me a contribution, but it's practically pocket change. If he's trying to impress me with his largesse, he's failed pretty miserably."

That earned her another laugh from Donovan. Then he casually tossed out a figure that nearly had her choking on her carrot. The St. James family—or maybe just Donovan—certainly put the riche in nouveau riche. When she could breathe again, she tried to sound just as casual. "Let's say I'm starting to feel impressed."

Donovan's white smile flashed in the moonlight. "Good."

"Now I've got to come up with another speech for tomorrow night. A similar yet different way to get a different set of people to open *their* checkbooks."

"Which group?"

"I'd have to check. The homeless shelter, maybe? It's at the convention center."

He shook his head. "That would be the Arts Association awards dinner. Not a fund-raiser for the homeless shelter."

Damn it. How did Vivi keep up with all of this? "Are you sure?"

"Quite. I'm supposed to be there."

Then when *was* the homeless-shelter event? She tried to picture Vivi's schedule… *Wait. Another* event where they'd both be there? That added a whole new dimension of conflict. It would be much easier to come to terms with her attraction to Donovan and the ramifications of that if she didn't have to face him.

"I guess I might see you there, then." *And sometime between now and then I'll figure out how I'm going to handle that.*

Donovan nodded before tossing a pizza roll into the air and catching it in his mouth. He looked at her expectantly.

It was the escape route she needed from confusing thoughts back into the fun surrealism of the evening. She applauded politely. "Nice trick. Now I am *really* impressed. You should have done that before you pledged money."

He picked up another. "Open your mouth," he said as he took aim.

"No way."

"Come on," he coaxed. "I'm trying to impress you, remember?"

Something about this seemed almost charming—which meant she either needed to get her head examined or else afterglow was even better than beer goggles. If anyone had tried to tell her that snide, pontificating pundit Donovan St. James would casually pledge an amount equal to an endowed chair at a university just seconds before trying to convince a woman to let him throw food at her, she'd have laughed in their face. But she hadn't seen the snide, pontificating pundit tonight. She didn't even really recognize the man in front of her as the Donovan she'd hated since high school.

No. Not hated. Just ignored and dismissed.

"Come on, Lorelei. Open up."

She shook her head. "If you miss I'll end up with sauce all over me."

"I never miss. Although I just might have to this time."

"Because…?"

He gave her a look that clearly said he'd be happy to lick her clean. It sent a naughty tingle all the way down to her toes. *Oh, why not?* Her proper upbringing frowned upon playing with one's food—much less tossing it at another human being—but hadn't she decided that tonight was outside the bounds anyway? Feeling foolish, she opened her mouth.

"Close your eyes."

"Why?"

"Because you'll flinch from it if you see it coming."

"Fine." She sighed and closed her eyes, then opened her mouth again.

"Tuck your chin in a little… Tilt your head a little to the left…"

She followed along like a puppet.

"Not that much… Okay, good."

It was amazingly quiet—quiet enough for her to hear the bubbles of the water in the pool. When nothing happened she started to get a little nervous. She kept her eyes closed, though, not wanting to end up with a pizza roll in them, but it was getting just a little awkward now.

A second later Donovan's mouth closed over hers. He caught her gasp of surprise, then his tongue swept in to tease hers.

"Sorry. Couldn't resist," he mumbled as he moved to her neck.

There was a small splash, and then Donovan was pulling her into the pool. The night was warm and muggy, and the water felt delicious lapping against her stomach. Somehow in those moments when she'd been waiting awkwardly, Donovan had lost his jeans, and she no longer minded being left to wait like that. The borrowed jersey floated up to her waist, allowing her bare skin contact with Donovan below the water's surface.

The contrast of warm skin and cool water, the tickle of hair against her thighs and stomach, and the heavy air above the refreshing water all combined with Donovan's kiss to send her senses into overload.

Oh, *yeah*. She was definitely impressed.

* * *

Once again Lorelei woke in a strange bed with a man sleeping beside her. Her brain was faster this time in making sense of the situation—and she lacked the massive hangover from last week—but the feeling of déjà vu couldn't be shaken.

Weak daylight peeked in around the curtains, telling her it was early yet. She could hear Donovan's deep, even breaths beside her, and one heavy leg had hers pinned to the bed. She was very glad Donovan was still asleep, otherwise this morning would end up being equally as awkward—but hopefully not as hostile—as the last time.

At least this time she remembered all the details—even if she was still a little fuzzy on the "why" part. Well, not completely fuzzy. She knew why she'd had sex with him: because she'd wanted to. Why she'd *wanted* to was a bit trickier to nail down.

It was all very confusing. And not something she really wanted to deal with right now.

Slowly and carefully, she slid her legs out from under his. Donovan mumbled and rolled over, but didn't wake, so she slipped out of the bed and took her clothing to the hallway to dress.

Once again she'd be going home in evening wear, but the chances of her being noticed were pretty slim, actually, since she knew which streets to avoid to keep accidental encounters to a minimum. Tiptoeing down the stairs, she grabbed the rest of her things. The sight of the alarm keypad next to the front door gave her pause. Had Donovan set the alarm last night?

Cringing the whole time, she opened the door and waited for sirens to blare and announce her exit. Nothing. With a sigh of relief she stepped outside, pulling the door closed and making sure it locked behind her. Cursing her footwear, she started the trek home.

It was early enough not to be miserable, but the day was already promising to be a scorcher, and the humidity was already high enough to have her hair sticking to her neck. She couldn't say the Quarter was waking up, since it never actually slept, but there were few people on the streets, and some of them looked worse than she did.

Normally the walk home wouldn't have taken more than fifteen minutes, tops, but her shoes slowed her down and that gave her more time to think. Pretty soon she was starting to wonder if bolting had been the best idea—and not just because her feet hurt.

Sneaking out like that made her feel as if she had done something wrong, something she regretted, and that really wasn't the case. But she was darned sure she didn't want to do the morning-after bit. Not with Donovan, at least. They'd agreed it was just about the sex, and she was okay with that, because she wasn't looking for anything more. She had too much on her plate at the moment to get involved with anyone beyond a physical thing. She needed to focus—not look for distractions—but she had to admit Donovan had been an excellent stress-reliever.

Even sweaty and sore-footed, she felt better than she had in quite a while. She'd needed last night, needed that release.

Her feet were dying as she got to the sidewalk in front of her house, and she slipped the shoes off before climbing the stairs to her porch. The blast of air-conditioning that greeted her felt even better. Dropping her stuff, she headed straight for the shower and then into bed.

As she closed her eyes she realized the stress relief hadn't been just physical. Last night's surrealism, that step

outside of the norm, had been exactly what she needed.
And that was all Donovan.

How very disturbing.

Yeah, she'd done the right thing by getting out of there.
She really didn't need the complication.

CHAPTER FIVE

LORELEI SMILED ALL THE way through the awards dinner, applauded politely as the names were called, and gave a simple yet heartfelt speech on Vivi's behalf as she received a plaque for her gallery's support of young and upcoming artists. Where Vivi would find room to hang the plaque was an excellent question, as the walls of her office were already lined with dozens of other awards of appreciation.

She ran her fingers over Vivi's name and felt a small twinge of regret. If only she could send a message back in time to her younger self, explaining how not all attention was good attention, that infamy was not the same as respect, and that there was such a thing as a permanent record—at least in people's minds—it might be her name on that plaque instead of Vivi's. *One day...*

She'd accepted the fact she'd never be the saint Vivi was a long time ago, but she was slowly making inroads, repairing the damage. This insane schedule had its benefits. She would have met pretty much every single important person in New Orleans by the time Vivi returned. Not that she didn't know them already, but there was a difference in knowing someone socially and seeing them as a professional. *That* was her goal.

They'd know her face—know her interest and her desire to serve.

She set Vivi's latest dust-catcher on the table in front of her and stifled a yawn. Functioning on about five hours of sleep was not easy—especially when that five hours hadn't been consecutive. She'd barely lain down for a much-needed nap this morning before her phone had started ringing. After running to the studio to sort out a problem, she'd barely gotten home in time to shower and come here. She could do Vivi's life or she could do hers. Doing both just might kill her.

Ten more days. She could make it ten more days.

Of course, she needed to make it through the next ten *minutes* without falling asleep first. Snoring on the table would make *such* a good impression, practically advertising to the world that she'd been out all night.

And, oh, what a night...

She felt herself starting to smirk and quickly reschooled her face into an expression of polite interest. Out of the corner of her eye, she scanned the ballroom. Donovan had said he might come, but she hadn't seen him yet.

That was probably a good thing. She wasn't a very good actress, and her little secret would be obvious to everyone. Since she was trying to live down a reputation—not enforce her old one—that would not be good. Plus she was still feeling a bit bad about sneaking out this morning without saying goodbye, and she still hadn't figured out how she was supposed to interact with Donovan now. They weren't friends, but they were certainly more than casual acquaintances. Who would have thought that things could get *more* awkward?

Yeah, she was very glad he wasn't here. She had a job to do, and thinking about last night would not make it any easier.

The awards and speeches finally ended, giving her the opportunity to get up and walk around. The movement helped wake her up, and shaking hands and making small talk proved boring but kept her alert. At the bar, she ordered a club soda.

Tipping the bartender, she turned to find Julie Cochran, who'd only recently moved back to town as she fought through a bitter and nasty divorce, right behind her.

"I'm fine," Julie insisted when Lorelei offered condolences—and alcohol, if needed.

When Julie exhaled, the Scotch on her breath told Lorelei she was a little late for that.

"The lying, cheating bastard is going to pay dearly for his inability to keep his pants on. My lawyer won't settle for less than a damn nice settlement and nearly half of his salary for my humiliation and pain."

She and Julie had never been particularly close, so this seemed like information she shouldn't be privy to. She wasn't quite sure how to respond. "Wow. Amazing. Remind me to call you if I ever need a recommendation for an attorney."

"Three words, sweetie. *Prenuptial agreement.* Make sure there's a penalty for adultery."

Lorelei wasn't sure if *prenuptial agreement* counted as three words or two, but she nodded anyway.

"Let me give you some more advice. Learn from my mistake. If a man is marrying up by marrying you, *run.* Dump him. He'll never truly respect you, and will only come to resent you for it."

That was a little more than expected. "I'll keep that in mind."

"Good." Julie patted her arm. "You're probably the exact person I needed to run into tonight. Now that I'm back home, I really need some help."

"Okay." This was normally the kind of thing people

went to her sister for, but Lorelei was pleased to step up. *Inroads, indeed.* "How can I help?"

"Point me toward the single men."

"Oh. Um…" That was unexpected. She glanced around the room. It wasn't as if the eligible bachelors traveled in packs or anything, to make them easier to hunt. "Anyone in particular?"

"I don't really care as long as he's young, handsome and rich. Preferably good in bed, too."

Lorelei nearly choked. To think Vivi was always accusing *her* of being too blunt or outrageous. Vivi would faint at Julie's words. *No, Vivi would handle it with aplomb.* "The first three are easier to deduce than the last, Julie."

"We'll start with the ones I know. Mike Devereaux?"

"Sorry, he's married."

"John Howard?"

"Married."

"Seth Ryland?"

"Gay."

Julie's eyebrows pulled together. "Really?"

Lorelei nodded.

"Well, that's a pity."

"Yeah."

"Kyle Hamilton?"

"The Hamiltons lost all their money in the last crash."

"Well, damn. Who *is* eligible?"

Lorelei scrambled for words as Julie ran through names like she was reading from the phonebook. This was getting quite uncomfortable. Even if she did have a viable suggestion, she'd feel dirty setting Julie loose on some unsuspecting man. Before she could come up with an answer, Julie grabbed her arm.

"Well, hel-*lo,* yummy goodness… Wait—is that Donovan St. James?"

Her head snapped to follow Julie's line of sight. He had come after all. The fluttery sinking of her stomach at seeing him was complicated by a stab of possessiveness at the open lust on Julie's face. She tried to keep her voice even. "Yes, it is."

"He's moving up nicely in the world. Who'd have thought it?"

Did Julie actually expect an answer?

The answer seemed to be no, as Julie moved on. "I've seen him on TV. He's much hotter in person and he ticks all my boxes nicely."

Now there was an uncomfortable stab of jealousy she didn't care to examine. "Julie…"

"Lord, I'm not going to marry him. I just want to—"

She coughed, not wanting to hear the details. Donovan was the one guy on Julie's list whose prowess Lorelei could attest to, and Julie was now drooling over him as if he was a tasty morsel she was ready to gobble up. Belatedly, she remembered Vivi saying Julie had always been a viperous bitch, but before she could extricate herself from the conversation and Julie's clutches gracefully, Julie was dragging her across the ballroom.

"Introduce us."

"You went to school with him for four years, Julie. You don't really need an introduction."

"But he wasn't Donovan St. James back then."

She dug her heels in and forced Julie to stop. "What?"

"Oh, you know what I mean."

Lorelei had the sneaking suspicion that she did. It was tacky and calculating on Julie's part. She didn't have time to mull about it, though, as they were now just feet from Donovan and she was not ready to face him just yet. She didn't have a plan in place. If there was ever a time to simply brazen through, now would be it.

To make things worse, Donovan was standing with Jack Morgan—possibly the only man Julie hadn't had on her list. But then, there was some kind of bad blood between Julie and Jack that went back to their prom as far as she could tell. That was just going to make this even more fun.

She plastered a smile on her face. "Jack. Donovan. Good to see you both tonight."

Donovan nodded at her, a short, sharp motion that implied complete uninterest in her, and her hackles went up a bit.

"That was a nice speech. Pass along my congratulations to your sister."

Jack was giving the same short, uncomfortable nod in Julie's direction, which she returned. *Well, this was just awkward all the way around.* Then he leaned in to kiss *her* cheek in greeting.

"Hi, there."

There was something a little too intimate in Jack's voice, and Lorelei felt like he was making a very premature claim with that kiss. She peeked at Donovan, but his face didn't so much as move. Granted, it would be strange if she and Donovan suddenly seemed all chummy, but still… It was just *wrong.*

Julie cleared her throat, and Lorelei remembered why she was standing here. "Sorry. Donovan—do you remember Julie Cochran?"

"Hebert," Julie corrected smoothly, extending her hand. "I've already taken back my name."

Donovan shot Lorelei a look that she didn't fully understand, but then turned to Julie. "From St. Katharine's. Of course."

Julie's smile turned downright lustful, and Lorelei tried to swallow the urge to snatch those blond extensions right off her head.

Where did that come from? It wasn't as if she had dibs on Donovan or something. And Donovan was pretty much treating her like a complete stranger. It was more than a little galling, but not exactly something she could call him on in the middle of a ballroom. *Especially* since Julie had stepped between them, effectively removing both Lorelei and Jack from the conversation.

Jack didn't seem to mind, though. He was now leaning in a little too close. "I tried to call you after you left last night."

She forced her attention away from Donovan and Julie. Speaking to Jack last night seemed so very long ago. "I know. Sorry. I was so exhausted by the time I got home I just crashed. I didn't get your message until this afternoon." That wasn't a flat-out lie: Jack didn't need to know that it had taken her over ten hours to go approximately ten blocks.

"So, when can I take you out to dinner?"

Okay, Jack was asking her out on a date while she was close enough to Donovan to smell his aftershave. The smell alone was sending little tremors down her inner thighs. Her life really was a farce.

"I'm pretty much totally booked up until Vivi and Connor get back from their honeymoon. It's a really crazy time."

"Then as soon as they get back, I want on your calendar."

Lorelei tried to smile and nod in a way that was polite without being committal.

"It must be tough for you. Stepping into Vivi's shoes like that."

Was that a jab? Or was she just oversensitive? *Damn, Donovan's scent was driving her insane.* "Vivi has fabulous shoes, and thankfully we wear the same size."

Julie threw her head back and laughed at something Donovan had said, and Lorelei was able to direct her attention to their conversation without seeming over-interested. She and Jack were being roundly excluded. In just a few minutes, Julie had moved in like an aircraft carrier, creating a no-fly zone around Donovan that said she'd shoot down any woman who dared come too close. Last night Jess; Julie tonight. Lorelei amended that list—first it had been Jess, then her, and now Julie. It seemed Donovan was a prime commodity these days. *He should get one of those "take a number" things.*

"Why don't we go refresh your drink?" Jack said. "I think these two have some catching up to do."

Lorelei nearly snorted. But Donovan wasn't exactly fighting off Julie's advances, and nor did he seem overly concerned with Jack's rather proprietary hovering.

Fine. She'd said last night that she didn't expect anything from him, and he seemed to be taking that at face value. Rationally, she had no real cause to be irritated about it. They were nothing at all to each other. Repeating that fact to herself, she let Jack guide her away.

She spent the next hour making polite conversation with all the right people, and playing slightly dumb to Jack's attempts to charm her straight into his bed. A week ago this would have been exactly what she wanted: the powerful and influential of New Orleans treating her as an equal player and a guy like Jack Morgan playing arm candy.

Jack Morgan: grandson of a former mayor, lawyer in his father's firm. She'd known him—or at least his family—her entire life. His mother and her mother were in several clubs together. Handsome, stable, well-liked, from a good family…Jack was *exactly* the kind of man everyone had expected her to pair up with. Just like every other girl she'd grown up with.

Vivi had almost bucked the rules by marrying a musician, but the Mansfields were literally the family next door—as old and established and respected as every other family in their social circle. No one had batted an eyelid when they'd ended up together.

She, though, had always dated outside her expected peer group—but she hadn't strayed too far, because she didn't want to give her grandmother a heart attack. She'd carefully chosen men just acceptable enough to protect her grandmother's heart, but also unacceptable enough to keep people from expecting her to get serious with any of them. It had been a careful balancing act designed to let her have the most amount of fun with the minimum amount of hassle. It was just easier that way.

And now there was Jack Morgan. Her mother would be thrilled.

Why wasn't *she* more thrilled?

Even examining him with a critical eye, she couldn't come up with a complaint. Jack was a good catch. But there was no tingle, no excitement at the thought.

Mentally she ran through Julie's recent list of eligible males, and found that none of them gave her even the slightest tingle.

Once again, the "right" thing held little or no interest for her. Hadn't that been the story of her life? And wasn't that exactly how she'd ended up here, hovering on the outskirts of her own society, trying to get back in like some high schooler who wanted to hang with the popular kids?

It was just downright depressing to contemplate.

Donovan revved her engines, but he was like tequila: not a good idea unless she wanted to make a fool of herself. As if she hadn't already made a big enough fool of herself by throwing herself at him last night.

And look what that had gotten her.

She looked over at Jack. Jack was exactly what she needed, tingle be damned.

The expectations of the right thing to do were ingrained into her: she was *supposed* to marry a man from the right family, have a couple of children to raise the right way, and settle into the society niche that had been carved for her at birth.

She'd tried, but she'd never quite measured up. And as Vivi had become the paragon of all the right virtues, she'd finally just given up even trying to live up to that standard and had become a bit of a rebel just out of a need for self-protection. She'd even convinced herself that she *wanted* to be the horrible warning instead of the good example.

Now, after years of not caring—or merely doing the minimum required of her—she found herself fighting for her place. She had a hell of a lot to prove to a hell of a lot of people, and the only way to accomplish that was by playing by their rules.

She sneaked a peek to her left. Donovan St. James was not in the playbook at all. *Pity.*

The problem with rebelling was that, while it was liberating and exciting, it painted her as an irresponsible flake who didn't respect the traditions she'd been taught her entire life. She'd been both an embarrassment and a disappointment to her family, because after failing to live up to Vivi's example she'd simply quit trying. If she harbored any hope of changing that now she not only had to live by the rules, she needed to embrace them and live them.

Vivi's honeymoon had handed her the perfect opportunity to show that she wasn't that girl anymore. This was a

crucial time for her; she couldn't afford a potentially embarrassing affair with Donovan.

Not that it seemed to be an option now, since Julie
seemed to have made her claim without a peep of pro-
test from Donovan. She should probably be happy Julie
had derailed that train before it could crash spectacularly.

A Lorelei-Donovan coupling—however brief and
non-permanent—would probably kill her grandmother.
Regardless of anything else he had going for him,
nothing—not the St. James family money, not even the
respect Donovan had earned in his profession—would
ever give Donovan St. James membership to the club as
long as the old guard were in power. And he probably still
wouldn't get an invite after they all died off, either. Some
lines just couldn't be crossed.

She might not fully agree with the attitude, but she was
so tired of being the family disappointment that she was
willing to do practically anything to change that. She'd
never be a pillar of that society, but she could at least be
a functioning member of it.

Damn. Now she was *really* depressed.

She signaled for a server and ordered a large glass of
wine.

I should not be chasing after Lorelei LaBlanc. It had been
an ordeal to get out of Julie Hebert's clutches—into which
Lorelei had delivered him in the first damn place, before
swanning off to spend the evening with Jack Morgan—
only to find out that Lorelei had left long ago, claiming
a headache.

Without saying goodbye. *Again.* Twice in one day was
just too much.

Honestly, he'd been a bit relieved when he'd woken to
an empty bed, as he had no idea how this morning would

have played out otherwise. Even though he could assume that Lorelei would have been much less huffy and antagonistic this time, there was no such thing as an *un*-awkward morning after. He was actually grateful that Lorelei had been so accommodating as to leave before the awkwardness set in and ruined the memory of a very pleasant night. Based on how adamant she'd been about leaving immediately last night, he rather assumed she felt the same way.

He had both respect for and experience with the fine art of the pre-dawn exit—so why, then, did he have a nagging irritation about Lorelei's? He'd done his fair share of bolting, but he'd at least tried *not* to make it look as if that was exactly what he was doing. And he never left without saying goodbye, even if he had to wake the woman up to do so, because not to would just be disrespectful. He liked to think he had better manners than *that*.

That was what ticked him off. And as the day had progressed it had only got worse. By the time he'd got to the awards dinner and seen Lorelei up on that stage...

Then, to make matters worse, she'd honed in on Jack Morgan like a heat-seeking missile—as if she hadn't been naked in *his* arms less than twelve hours earlier.

He'd known hooking up with Lorelei was insanity.

Yet here he was, navigating his way through the pedestrians that spilled out of the clubs on Frenchman Street on his way to her house. He hadn't phoned first—even after two nights spent tangled in her arms he still didn't have her number—but he knew exactly where she lived thanks to Connor and Vivi's press.

The one thing he didn't know yet was exactly *why* he had this need to track her down tonight. It could backfire spectacularly in his face, but even that knowledge didn't have him turning around. Damn, he was a glutton for punishment.

He found a spot on the street about a block from her house and parked. The streets weren't well lit, and jazz from one of the clubs floated on the air, broken only by the occasional laugh or shout of party-goers down the street.

Lorelei's house sat close to the road, with only a small strip of grass separating the sidewalk from a wide, screened-in wraparound porch. Most of the house was dark: only one light inside and one on the porch glowed against the night. He remembered Lorelei saying something about a roommate who was never home, and hoped that would be the case tonight.

As he turned up the walk he wasn't surprised to see Lorelei reclined lengthwise across a large wooden swing, head back against a cushion. She held a tablet in one hand, the steady movement of one finger scrolling through whatever was on the screen. One bare foot touched the wood planks, keeping the swing gently in motion.

When Lorelei heard his steps, she sat up and stopped the swing. The sparkly cocktail dress had been replaced with a pair of cut-offs that exposed the long sleek lines of her thighs and a tank top that clearly outlined her breasts—and advertised the fact she wasn't wearing a bra. That mass of hair was pulled up and clipped to the back of her head to keep her cool. She'd looked glamorous and sexy-as-hell earlier, but somehow the simplicity of this outfit had a powerful effect on him. His blood rushed south so fast he got a little light-headed. Even if his brain wasn't sure why he was here, his body damn sure was.

"Well, this is a surprise. What brings you by?" Lorelei didn't move from the swing, so he was left standing on the other side of the screen door.

He shrugged. "You left rather suddenly. People were concerned."

Lorelei set the tablet aside and reached for the beer bottle on the table beside her. "And so you decided to come check on me?"

"Seemed like I should. Hasty or stealthy exits usually mean something isn't right."

She nodded. "*Uh-hmm.* Well, my business was finished. No sense sticking around."

"Obviously."

Lorelei shook her head. "So *that's* the bee in your bonnet? Seriously?"

"Excuse me?"

"Let's not play games."

"That would be refreshing."

"You told me to lock the door behind me when I left. I did. You were still asleep, and I saw no reason to wake you and go through a weird morning-after pantomime. It wasn't some kind of statement." She laughed. "I had no idea your ego was so fragile."

God, she had the most amazing ability to twist everything. "My ego is *not* fragile."

An eyebrow went up, mocking him. "Really? Then why are you here?"

That caught him off guard, and he realized he was acting *exactly* as if that was the problem. It was just as ridiculous as it sounded, and while his earlier irritation wouldn't quite go away, it no longer seemed like a big deal. With that knowledge, the *other* reason driving him came rushing back to the forefront, causing his zipper to dig into his skin.

"This is the one place Julie Hebert won't think to look for me."

Lorelei bit her bottom lip, but he could tell she was trying not to laugh. She finally got off the swing and came to unlatch the screen door.

"You should be flattered. Julie has a list of requirements, and you were the only one who met all the criteria."

"Upright and breathing?"

If she bit her lip any harder she would draw blood. "They were a little more stringent than that."

"Fat checkbook?"

She shrugged. "That might have been on the list."

"Then spare me the rest of her criteria. I don't want to know."

She reached under the table and he heard ice rattling. "Beer?" She had one out and was holding it in his direction before he could even answer.

That was a good sign. He accepted the bottle and sat in the wicker rocker on the other side of the table as she went back to the swing. "Well, if you struck out tonight it's your own fault. Julie was certainly willing."

Was that jealousy he heard in her voice? "Did you not hear the part about me finding a place where Julie wouldn't look?"

"Well, this would be the right place. Julie Hebert and I aren't exactly friends."

"So you set her loose on *me?* Gee, thanks."

Lorelei might have smiled as she curled one leg up into the swing with her and used the other foot to put it in motion again. He liked how easily Lorelei seemed to get past things, without holding grudges or needing to discuss it to death. She might flare up easily, but once it was done, it was done, it seemed. It made things…comfortable.

Beside her, the glowing screen of the tablet went dark.

"Working?"

"The event for the homeless shelter is on Monday, as it turns out. I'm trying to prepare. Vivi's assistant sent over some notes, but…"

"Vivi had better watch out. Little sis will be showing her up, taking her title."

"Oh, I don't want her title. One saint is enough for any family."

"You're probably right."

Her head fell back. "I'll be so glad when they're back from their honeymoon. Her schedule is insane."

"Vivi makes it look easy."

"I know. It's been a humbling experience, to say the least."

"But I bet Vivi doesn't have time to sit on the porch and enjoy a beer on a summer night."

Lorelei conceded that with a nod. "She doesn't. But then porch-sitting and beer-drinking aren't the best use of my education or a productive use of my time. Privilege entails us to responsibility. I should be setting a good example."

Well, *that* was a loaded statement if ever he'd heard one, but Lorelei had delivered it without bitterness or sarcasm. She sounded more resigned than anything else. He watched her closely and decided the beer in her hand was not her first one of the evening. She wasn't drunk, but she was certainly unguarded.

He heard a ping and Lorelei reached for her phone. A glance at the screen had her snorting. "Julie may not think to look for you here, but she's definitely looking for you. She's texted me to see if I know how to get in touch with you."

"Please say no."

She frowned at the screen. "I'm trying to figure out how she got *my* number."

"I imagine it was quite easy for her. You both know all the same people."

"But I actually don't have your number, so it's not a lie

if I tell her that." Lorelei put the phone down and leaned back again. "You know she just wants you for sex?"

"That was made very clear, yes."

"And that doesn't bother you?"

There was a certain irony in her question, considering their situation. "Not really." He caught her eyes and held them. "As long as both parties are clear on the rules, I don't see the harm."

Lorelei seemed to think about that. "Maybe," she said, in the most non-committal tone he'd ever heard.

"I will admit that I'm rather surprised to be on her list, though."

"Why?"

"After listening to her tirade against her low-class, social-climbing ex-husband, I would have thought she'd limit her rebound choices to someone with a better pedigree."

"Charming. You make us sound like we're registered with the kennel club."

"Honestly, you sort of *are*. Got to protect those bloodlines."

Lorelei leveled a look at him. "I'll admit there's some of that going on."

"Just 'some'?"

Lorelei made a face. "I don't know quite how to say this nicely...but you do know that it's you *personally* that's the problem, right?"

At least she was willing to be honest about it. "There's a problem?" he joked.

"Oh, please. You destroyed two families—"

"I didn't destroy anyone or anything. I just happened to be the one who found out and exposed the whole dirty mess."

"Oh, *I* know that. But, say what you like about pedigrees, we are a loyal bunch. We protect and defend our own."

"Closed ranks?"

"Exactly. You're looking at families, businesses and relationships that go back generations, so we're all tied together. I know these people—have known them my entire life. I can't help but feel for them."

"It's not that I don't feel for those families, but Lincoln DuBois made his family vulnerable by the choices he made."

"No one believes that what Mr. DuBois was doing was right, but it still sent a shock wave through our community. And *you* were the cause of that shock wave."

"You think I did those articles with an ulterior motive?"

She gave a half shrug, half nod that said an awful lot.

"What motive could I possibly have?"

"A search for glory and fame, maybe? You certainly got both of those. Then there's the possibility of spite or jealousy? A chance to bring down people you envy?" Lorelei shrugged. "I'll admit I thought that way for a while."

He didn't know what to say to that.

"I'm just telling you that, right or wrong, you brought this on yourself. You can't take on the big dogs and not expect to get bitten. Like I said, the pack is loyal."

Just as she dropped that bomb her phone pinged again, cutting off his chance to respond as she grabbed it and read the text. Once again, her attitude changed completely as she laughed at whatever was on the screen.

"Sorry."

Before he would question her apology, his own phone started to ring.

As he fished it out of his pocket Lorelei said, "I wouldn't answer that if I were you. Not if you want to remain unfound tonight."

"Really? Julie got my number *that* quickly?"

"Never underestimate what a woman will do—especially when she's horny. I'd be careful with Julie Hebert, though. Even Vivi doesn't like her, and Vivi likes everybody."

He sent the call to voice mail. "I don't understand you at all, Lorelei."

"So few do." She chuckled. "But then that makes us even. I don't get you, either."

"I'm not exactly a mystery. What you see is what you get."

She looked at him closely, then shook her head. "No. I don't think so."

"What makes you say that?"

"The fact you're on my porch."

Once again the quick change in topic had him scrambling to catch up. *Boy, Lorelei really didn't want to play games.* "Think about it for a second. That's not really a great mystery, either."

She gave him a smile that made him want to take her right there, on the swing, without giving a single damn about who might see. "At least you're honest about it."

"Do you want me to lie?"

"Nah. If I want sunshine blown up my skirt I'll call Jack." She raised an eyebrow at him. "Do you know I'm the most *fascinating* woman he's ever met?"

There was that strange need to punch Jack again. "Actually, I would agree."

"Oh, so you *can* do empty flattery?"

"No, it's just I've met most of the same women. The competition isn't that stiff."

"Ouch." She shook her head. "If that's your pickup line, no wonder you're still single."

"So are you."

"*That* took careful planning on my part, my friend. The kennel club is all about selective breeding, you know, so I stay far away from the prize studs."

It was his turn to laugh at her. "The mutts are much more interesting anyway."

She grinned back and took another drink. They sat there in silence for a few moments, but it wasn't an uncomfortable silence. And that was kind of odd.

But it was nice, too.

Then Lorelei sighed. "Don't take this personally, but I think you should go."

"What?" How was he *not* supposed to take that personally?

"If you stay, I'm probably going to invite you inside."

He didn't actually see the problem with that, but Lorelei's voice was so heavy, *she* obviously did. "And here I was kind of hoping you would."

She sighed. "Two hook-ups make a fling. Three hook-ups… Well, then it starts to become something. And this isn't supposed to *be* something."

And he was a mutt. "'Something' is a mighty big category. Lots of room for interpretation."

Her chin lifted as she considered that. "True. Something doesn't have to be anything. I'm just not sure what, if anything, *this* something could be. Everything is so complicated right now that a something that's not anything might be a good thing. Or nothing. Or something like that."

He'd lost the thread of this conversation pretty quickly, causing him to rethink his earlier assessment of her sobriety. "How much have you had to drink, Lorelei?"

She laughed and ran a hand over her face. "That didn't make much sense, did it? But it's not alcohol. I'm more tired than anything else. I didn't get much sleep last night."

"Neither did I, now that you mention it."

"Can I ask you something?"

"Sure."

"I know why you're here, but I want to know why you're here instead of at Julie Hebert's. Or Jess Reynald's, for that matter."

"You're prettier, for one thing."

She frowned at him. "Honestly, now."

He'd had another flippant answer, but at that qualifier he swallowed it. "Jess and Julie have agendas. I don't like being an item on an agenda. Or a means to an end, either."

"I thought we were clear that Julie was just wanting to use you for sex?"

"If she were just looking for a good time, that would be one thing. But Julie's on the rebound and angry with it. I'm not about to get pulled into that. She'd just be using me to get back at her soon-to-be-ex. Jess's agenda is a bit more complex, but both of them are playing games and I don't play."

"So you assume I don't have an agenda?"

"Oh, you have an agenda, too. Whatever you're out to prove right now by taking over for Vivi." The look that passed over her face told him he'd hit a nerve there and confirmed his suspicions. "I'm obviously not a part of the plan. You wouldn't be so worried about 'everything' otherwise."

"How astute of you." Although it was politely enough said, a barrier dropped between them at that moment. "In fact, you would be—*are*," she corrected, "a big old monkey wrench in my plans. Which is why this can't be something."

"I respect the fact you're honest enough with your-self—and me—to say that. Of course that also means that you're honest enough to take this for what it is—*without* it becoming something or anything beyond that."

"Wow." She blew out her breath and shook her head. "I'm not sure if I should be flattered or insulted."

"Neither, actually. You asked for honesty."

"And it seems like I got it."

With another deep sigh, Lorelei stood and stretched. Maybe honesty hadn't been the best policy. Maybe he'd read this situation wrong. Of course if he had, and Lorelei had been looking for some other answer, it was probably a good thing he'd found out now, instead of later. It was disappointing, but...

"I'm going to bed." Lorelei picked up the tablet from the swing and grabbed her beer from the table.

Well, he had his answer. "Good night."

Lorelei paused with her hand on the door. "Are you coming?"

CHAPTER SIX

"LORELEI, HONEY, PLEASE sit up straight. I hate it when you slouch."

Mom hated so many things: slouching, chewing gum, Lorelei's hair in her face, white shoes after Labor Day… Lorelei pushed herself upright and wrapped another pink ribbon around the top of the prize bag she was making for one of her mother's friend's daughter's baby showers. "Sorry, Mom. I'm just a little tired today."

"I'm not surprised. The way you've been kept running between Connor's studio and Vivi's gallery and all of those meetings and things…I've barely seen you all week."

It was true that she'd been busy, and if her mom wanted to assume it was just because Connor and Vivi were out of town that was all for the good. Lorelei saw no need to enlighten her to anything different. Mom did not need to know about her extracurricular activities. That was a little secret she was keeping totally to herself. It was the only thing keeping her sane. Donovan was an excellent stress-reliever—not only physically, but mentally, as well. He made a good sounding board and a sympathetic ear. He was also pretty damn good for her ego, and her ego needed all the boosting it could get these days.

"Sarah Jenson told me about the speech you gave at the

Women's Leadership lunch. I'm sorry I couldn't be there to hear it myself. She said it was very good."

"Thanks. Vivi gave me the theme, but I was pretty pleased with how it turned out."

"Well, I couldn't be prouder. I knew you had it in you. It just took you a little longer to settle in."

Lord, it was like being handed a long-stemmed rose and being expected to smile while the thorns shredded your skin. Lorelei just nodded and unspooled another eighteen inches of pink ribbon. Five more to make and then she could probably escape, while still remaining in her mother's good graces for the help.

"Speaking of…"

Mom started in a casual tone, and Lorelei's antennae twitched. Her mom's casual tone meant the topic was anything but casual.

"I hear that Jack Morgan asked you to dinner."

The connection between Sarah Jenson, the Women's Leadership luncheon and Jack Morgan was as clear as mud, but she'd let it pass. "How'd you hear that?"

"Jack mentioned it to his mother, and Dorothy told me."

Why on earth would Jack tell his mother? "He did, actually."

"And…?"

"And I told him that I was completely booked until Vivi got back into town, but that we'd talk about it then."

"You'll 'talk about it?' Lorelei…"

"Mom, you just said yourself how busy I am. It's not like I turned him down flat or anything. I just want to focus on what I've already got on my plate. There'll be plenty of time for dinners after Vivi gets back and I've had a chance to recuperate."

"Fine. I just wanted you to know that I think it's a wonderful idea. Jack is an excellent catch."

"What does Mrs. Morgan think?" She couldn't keep the sarcasm out of her voice, but her mom didn't call her on it.

"Dorothy's willing to move past all of that now."

"I should hope so. It's been almost ten years." Mrs. Morgan had been president of the St. Katharine's parent-teacher association when Lorelei's freshman class had disagreed with an edict regarding the winter formal. While official blame had never been cast, and nothing had ever been proved, Mrs. Morgan still gave Lorelei that *look* every time she saw her. "It's not like her garden didn't benefit in the long run," Lorelei added quietly. "Manure is an excellent fertilizer."

Her mom frowned and shook her head, effectively changing the subject. "So, when you 'talk about' dinner with Jack, are you going to say yes?"

Damn it. She was losing brownie points now with this conversation. "I don't know, Mom. We'll see."

"Why, honey? What's wrong with Jack?"

"Nothing that I know of." That much was true. Jack was perfect on paper, but while there was nothing *wrong* with him, she was coming up with few reasons why he would be *right.* There was no good way to say that to her mother, though, because she really doubted Mom wanted to hear about tingling or the lack thereof where Jack was concerned. "I mean, I don't really know him all that well."

"And that's what first dates are for."

Mom had stayed out of her love life for the most part, but Vivi's engagement and wedding had her hyperaware at the moment. Maybe it would pass soon.

"I just wish that tacky woman hadn't started that rumor about you in the paper."

"It's not even a rumor, Mom. It was an observation— and it's not false. I *did* hang out in the bar until the wee hours of the morning."

That earned her a frown for her behavior. "But she made it sound tawdry. Which was not the best—"

"Yet I seem to be doing just fine regardless. The rumor didn't stick, and no one has brought it up in over a week." In an attempt to change the subject before Donovan's name actually came up, Lorelei said, "And did you see the write-up in yesterday's paper about the Children's Music Project?"

"Yes, and what a good picture. That purple dress was a good choice. It looked very nice on you."

Donovan had said almost the same thing late last night, when they'd sat in the pool in his courtyard. Only he'd added, "It looked even better on my bedroom floor…" with a grin and a leer. Lorelei kept her eyes on the slippery ribbons, hoping Mom would think she was concentrating on the prize bag and not notice the smirk she was trying to keep in check.

"In fact I'm thinking about looking for something for me in a similar color for your father's retirement dinner. What do you think?"

Since Lorelei had inherited her mother's looks—looking at Mom was the next best thing to a mirror with a portal to the future—any color that worked on her would work on her mother, too. "I think you'd look fabulous."

"Your father and I are going to the Delacroixes' for dinner tonight. You've been invited to join us if you're not busy."

"I don't know, Mom. There's nothing on the schedule for tonight, and I think I should probably leave it that way. Maybe have a quiet night and go to bed early."

"That's a good idea. A night in every now and then is good for your mental health. Take a long, hot bath and curl up with a good book."

"That certainly sounds like a good plan." *Her* plan,

though, was much better: she was picking up Thai food on her way to Donovan's, and while she'd go to bed early it would be not be to sleep, and she certainly wasn't curling up with a book. The bath idea held promise, though...

She tied the last ribbon and fluffed the bow. "Anything else you need, Mom, before I go?"

"Already?"

"I've got some phone calls to make and emails to sort through."

"I almost miss the days when you weren't so busy."

"Ah, but in those days you were after me to do something productive. Now I am."

"And I'm so pleased. Enjoy your night. Will Callie be joining you? A girls' night in?"

Lorelei coughed. "No. Callie is really busy with exams and things." And she was quite thankful for that. It made Lorelei's coming and goings at odd hours less noticeable.

Leaving her mom's with a sigh of relief—and one of exasperation, too—she went straight to the studio on Julia Street. The receptionist was reading a magazine. She wasn't the only one with a lighter workload while Connor was gone. Lorelei sent her home early, saying that she would watch the phones while she worked.

ConMan was normally a hive of activity, with musicians coming in and out of the recording studios while their entourages milled around the reception area and the phones rang off the hook, so the silence and stillness felt eerie.

That was a blessing, though, because she really did have a ton of emails and phone calls to deal with—including another one from Vivi, who wanted an update on how things were going. Vivi just couldn't let go. Instead of the detailed report she knew Vivi wanted, she chuckled and just typed, *All is well. Enjoy your honeymoon.*

The other emails and phone calls were easily dispatched, except for a couple that Connor would have to deal with, but Lorelei still hadn't received a text from Donovan, telling her he was home from today's round of televised punditry. She paid a few bills, did a little busy work around Connor's office, even shopped online for a wedding gift for Vivi since she hadn't found time to get one before.

Still no text from Donovan. It was now an hour past the time he'd said he'd be done, and she didn't know if she should be worried or just plain angry. Where the hell was he? Technically, where he was when he wasn't with her wasn't her business, but they'd made plans, and common courtesy required that Donovan contact her to let her know if the plans had changed. An hour wasn't just "a little late." An hour crossed into "stood up" territory. She called his phone, but it rolled straight to voice mail. She hung up without leaving a message.

Screw it. This was just plain rude and she wasn't going to put up with that.

She turned off the lights in the studio offices as she gathered her things, safe in the knowledge that she had every right to be angry and the steam coming out of her ears was completely justifiable.

What didn't make sense was that she felt a little hurt. Shrugging that off, she focused on being mad instead.

She checked her watch in disgust. She'd waited so long to hear from Donovan she'd now have to sit in rush-hour traffic and fume. By the time she was three blocks from home she was really good and mad—and of course that was the moment Donovan finally decided to call.

She was half tempted to ignore his call, but decided she'd rather give him a piece of her mind instead.

Donovan opened with an apology. "So sorry."

"For what?" she asked with as much innocence as she could. She was *not* going to give Donovan the idea that she actually cared one way or the other.

"Did you not hear about the scandal breaking in Baton Rouge today?"

"No, I've been really busy today." That wasn't a lie; she'd accomplished quite a bit.

"I was already in the studio when the news broke, and suddenly every network needed a talking head. It was insane. By the time I could catch my breath my battery was dead—"

She parked, turned off the ignition and climbed out. The sweltering heat hit her like a wall and didn't help her mood any. "Sounds like you were quite busy."

"I am sorry, though. I saw you called, but—"

The lame apologies were not going to work. "Your battery was dead. I know."

"Well, I'm finally done and I'm starving. You ready?"

"Sorry, Donovan." She tried to inject just the right note of insincere disappointment into her voice. "When I didn't hear from you I made other plans for tonight."

"I see." The words were clipped.

Where did he get off, acting like this? *She* was the one who had the right to be annoyed about this. She didn't need this kind of crap from him. "Good." She opened the door and stepped into the cool air of her house.

There was a brief silence before Donovan sighed. "You're mad at me."

There was no reason to lie. "Yeah."

"I apologized."

"And I appreciate that. Doesn't change things, though. It's simply good manners to call when you're going to be late."

"My battery was dead."

"And no one else had a phone? There wasn't a single phone in the entire building? Wow, that changes everything."

"Lorelei…"

"Don't. Look, I'm not your mother, so I'm not asking for an accounting of your time. I just expect a little respect for mine."

"Duly noted."

"Good. Now, I'm going to let you go and get on with my night. Bye, Donovan." Disgusted, she dropped her phone back into her purse and flopped onto the couch.

That hadn't been her best, most mature moment ever—but, damn it, she had the right to expect basic levels of human respect. She wasn't some booty call he got to make when it suited him.

Of course she now felt as if she'd cut off her nose to spite her face. Her stand for principle meant she was now going to spend the evening alone.

Yeah, her pride was a problem. She'd meant to draw a boundary and might have burned the bridge instead. She should have just let it go.

Bath, book, bed. It wouldn't kill her. She'd start with a glass of wine.

Donovan stared at his phone. Had she really just hung up on him? Because he was late and hadn't had time to call? He'd been *working,* for God's sake, not just playing around. Some people had *actual* jobs, *real* responsibilities that took precedence over a social calendar. Did she expect him just to stop in the middle of what he was doing to call her? It wasn't as if he'd blown her off completely; he'd called as soon as he could.

But it seemed that wasn't good enough. Good Lord, Lorelei needed a taste of life outside her little bubble before she got all high-and-mighty about tardiness.

Rush-hour traffic only increased his temper, and by the time he got home his mood was downright foul. He turned on the TV, grabbed a drink and settled in to watch a race, but it bored him pretty quickly. Eyeballing his laptop, he decided he would work a little, but for the first time ever, work didn't hold any appeal, either.

Mainly because deep down he'd rather be doing something else. And the realization that he wanted to do that something else with Lorelei was a bit of a shocker.

I'm not asking for an accounting of your time. I just expect a little respect for mine.

It's simply good manners.

Lorelei did have a point, he admitted. This was new territory for him. He preferred casual relationships for that exact reason: casual was easier. Lorelei was—or was supposed to be—even *more* casual, but for some reason he couldn't dismiss her words.

Which also meant he couldn't dismiss her anger, and he had to admit it was justified. Which put him in the wrong—a place he wasn't used to being.

Why did it bother him so much?

With a sigh, he reached for the phone and called in a favor.

To his relief, his phone rang forty-five minutes later.

"How on earth did you manage to get flowers delivered at this time of night?"

At least she wasn't mad enough to ignore the delivery. "I know people."

"I know people, too, you know."

"Yes, but *I* know the kind of people who own flower shops and owe me favors."

He heard her snort. "Seems like a waste of a perfectly good favor."

"Not really. I'm pretty sure flowers are the standard opening salvo for making amends."

"Well, they're lovely. But you're still in trouble."

He reminded himself that Lorelei wasn't one to hold a grudge. He just needed to get her past *this*. The fact she was talking to him, even giving him flak over the flowers, was actually a pretty good sign.

"So I'll apologize again. You were right. I was being very rude. I assure you I was raised better than that." When Lorelei stayed silent on her end, he added, "I'm not used to being accountable for my whereabouts to anyone else. At least not since I moved out of my parents' house."

"Well, that's quite a proper apology."

He could hear her giving in. "Nothing's more irritating than a non-apology apology, and I've ripped enough of those apart to make me a hypocrite if I tried it."

"You're assuming I'd fall for a lame non-apology apology?"

"Not at all. I respect you too much for that."

"Really?" She sounded skeptical.

"Of course. We couldn't be friends otherwise."

There was a pause. "Is that what we are? Friends?"

He hadn't really thought about it until now, but it had a nice ring to it. "I'd like to think so."

"I'm good with that, actually. Your apology is accepted."

He couldn't quite name the feeling that settled in his chest. There was relief, but there was something else, too. "So, are you ready for dinner now?"

"Yeah."

He was already reaching for his shoes. "I'll pick you up in about fifteen minutes."

"That's not necessary."

Before he could question that his doorbell rang. "Hang on for a second."

Opening the door, he found Lorelei on his stoop.

She smiled and put her phone back in her purse. "Hey."

He leaned against the doorframe. "So all of that was just to string me along?"

"No. I was willing to accept your apology even before the flowers arrived. I figured I'd save some time."

"So we're good now?"

"Yeah, I think we are."

He stepped back to let her in, and she smiled as she passed. She dropped her bag as he closed the door. "Are you really hungry? Like starving?"

"I can probably hang on for a little while longer."

"Good." Lorelei put her hands on his waist and rose up to her tiptoes until her mouth was just inches from his. "I think we need to kiss and make up first."

"What is up with the male fascination with gadgetry?" Lorelei scowled at his remote control. "This thing has more buttons than the cockpit of the space shuttle."

Donovan was replying to an email from his editor as Lorelei cursed at the remote. He looked up long enough to see her make a face at it and said, "The five buttons at the top are pretty much all you need."

"Then why does it have five-hundred buttons?"

He hit Send and laid the phone on the table. "I said those five at the top were the only ones *you'd* need. *I* know what the other four hundred and ninety-five do."

"Never mind. I've now forgotten what I wanted to watch." She tossed the remote to the other end of the couch. Remnants of Thai delivery food covered the coffee table, and Lorelei was nursing a glass of wine.

All in all it was a very casual, very comfortable, very laid-back evening—not something he was normally accustomed to. That should make the situation *un*comfortable, but for some reason it didn't. Over the last couple of days they'd settled into...well, not a routine, but a zone. An easy, comfortable zone. They spent their days doing their own thing, and their evenings doing something else. But it wasn't just All Sex, All The Time; they'd spent most of tonight on separate laptops, him working on an op-ed piece and her sending emails or something.

"I thought you had a big meeting to prepare for?"

"I do. But it's not like I have to cram for it."

"Why?"

"I'm starting to get the hang of this—finally. Fifty percent of it is just showing up, smiling and listening. That doesn't require much prep on my part. I'm very good at showing up and smiling."

He patted her leg. "It's good that you've found your true talent."

She stuck out her tongue at him. "You know, I've found that no one really likes it when someone just shows up and just starts bloviating endlessly, subjecting everyone to their opinion whether they want to hear it or not."

"I'm paid to bloviate, thank you very much."

She snorted. "Doesn't mean it will win you friends and help you influence people."

"I've got all the friends I need," he countered.

"God, you're cocky."

He just shrugged as Lorelei settled herself into the corner of the couch with her glass of wine and draped her legs over his. She had on jeans and another tank top, and her bare feet rested on his thigh. Her toenails were painted an electric shade of blue.

"Blue?" he asked.

She wiggled her toes in response. "I like it."

"It's just a little unexpected."

She shot him a grin. "I'm a rebel, don't you know?"

"With those toes? Of course you are. Everyone better watch out."

"Hey, I quietly rebel in my own way." The grin turned conspiratorial. "It's easier to look like I'm playing by the rules when I know that secretly I'm really not. It keeps me sane."

The differences between the new-and-improved public Lorelei LaBlanc and the private woman on his couch were getting starker each day. "I knew you hadn't turned over a completely new leaf."

"I'm just picking my battles more carefully these days."

"Why?"

She shrugged. "Everyone has to grow up sometime."

"I'm not seeing the connection."

She thought for a moment and sighed. "Have you never gotten tired of fighting something and decided it was easier to give in?"

It seemed he'd spent years not giving in. Not personally, not professionally. He wouldn't be here now if he had. Fighting the odds and succeeding was his heritage; his family tree consisted of sharecroppers and madams in Storyville, and now they were one of the wealthiest families in New Orleans. Backing down wasn't an option. "Not if the battle is worth it."

"And that's why I'm choosier with my battles these days. Some things will never change, so if I can't beat them I might as well join them."

"Such a cynical attitude from one so young."

Lorelei lifted her chin. "It's working, though. After my speech at that Women's Leadership luncheon, one of the Mayor's aides asked me to serve on a new task force."

"What kind of task force?"

"Honestly, I'm not sure. Something with schools, maybe?"

"And you agreed without knowing for sure?"

She nodded. "I was just so pleased she'd asked, yeah."

"My sister told me you gave a great speech. Obviously she wasn't the only one who thought that."

Lorelei pulled her legs in towards her chest and leaned forward. "I didn't know you had a sister."

"Caroline. And two brothers. David and Matt."

"Why didn't I know that?" Her eyebrows pulled together as if she was confused. "Did they go to St. Katharine's?"

"No. I'm the youngest by several years, so even if they had you probably wouldn't have known them." He was going to leave it there, but something had him saying, "Back then my parents couldn't afford the tuition for fancy prep schools. I was only at St. Katharine's because of a partial scholarship."

Understanding crossed her face. "Things changed quickly for you, though?"

"That they did." That was when he'd learned that being poor was far more acceptable than suddenly coming into money. The poor were treated with pity, but the nouveau riche were treated with suspicion and scorn. It had been a rude awakening.

Lorelei nodded. "I remember."

"Really?"

"Of course. Everyone was talking about it."

He'd known, of course, that people had talked—not to him, of course, because that wasn't the way it was done—but he didn't like being reminded of it.

"Didn't your father endow something shortly after that?"

He nodded. "A scholarship fund for other students." It had been too late for Donovan's siblings to benefit scholastically from their new wealth, and his folks had always regretted that fact. "Actually, we have scholarship funds in place at all the area private schools."

"Need or merit?"

"Both."

She smiled approvingly. "That's really great."

"You sound surprised."

"Not surprised," she corrected. "Pleased. People often forget to give back."

"Listen to you. Two weeks as the mini-Vivi and you know all the right things to say."

A frown crossed her face.

"What?"

"I'm not a mini-Vivi, and I don't want to be."

He hadn't meant it as an insult, but he'd hit a nerve nonetheless. "Isn't that what you're doing?"

"No. I'm just taking advantage of Vivi being out of the country. I score higher when she's not around for comparison."

"You sound bitter."

"I'm not."

Disbelief must have shown on his face, because Lorelei became emphatic.

"I'm *not.* Vivi is amazing, and I truly respect and admire her. It's just that she's set the bar so darn high it's impossible for anyone to measure up when she's around."

So many things made sense now. "And that's what you're trying to do?"

"It's what I *am* doing," she said, sitting up straighter. A note of pride entered her voice. "And it's working. I filled in for Vivi at the Women's Leadership luncheon, but it was *my* speech. *I* got offered the place on the task force. I don't think they offered it only because Vivi wasn't available. It's just that everyone in this town is so accustomed to going straight to Vivi that they don't think about asking someone else. Someone else who might be able to do just as good a job. Maybe even a *better* job because her time isn't as parceled out already."

She had a point, but… "That's what you want? To end up like Vivi eventually?"

"You say that like it's a bad thing," she said with a laugh.

"It's not the best."

The laugh died and the smile disappeared. "Vivi is loved and respected by everybody." Her hackles were up in defense of her sister.

"Nothing against your sister—you know I think she's great—but this city is doing its very best to suck her dry. Everyone loves a workhorse because they don't want to be the one doing the work, and everyone respects those who serve others. It's like nuns."

She'd been nodding in agreement until that last sentence. "Nuns?"

"You respect nuns, right?"

"Of course. Who doesn't?"

"Care to join a convent?"

Lorelei choked on her wine and coughed hard.

"I'll take that as a no. But if you're after respectability you should probably consider it. It might be easier for you in the long run."

She leaned back against the arm of the couch in a provocative pose. "Do you think I'm nun material?"

He let his eyes roam slowly over her. "No."

Lorelei returned the appraisal. "Good."

"But as far as I can tell there's very little you can actually do to change people's minds about you."

The femme fatale disappeared as Lorelei huffed in exasperation. "I disagree. You only have to prove them wrong."

"Oh, because that *always* works."

"*Now* who sounds bitter?" she challenged.

"Resigned, not bitter. There's a difference."

"Not really. I will concede that it's hard to do—".

"Exactly—"

"*But,*" she continued, talking over him, "it's not impossible. Case in point—I thought you were a conceited, blow-hard jerk."

He liked sparring with her. "And you still do."

"Because it's mostly true," she countered.

"I am not a blow-hard. I'm a respected pundit and journalist."

"Whatever." She waved a hand. "But since that's what you show the world, what do you expect? I speak from personal experience here. Act like a flaky rebel—be treated like a flaky rebel. It's hard to live down a reputation, but it's not impossible."

"Um…hate to break it to you, but your reputation is 'spoiled brat with a wild streak,' not 'flaky rebel.'"

Her jaw dropped. "Not true."

"True."

A snort escaped before she caught herself and re-schooled her face into a picture of dismay. "Then I'm screwed, because that's actually the truth."

"You don't say?"

"I might actually have to join a convent if I want to counter *that* label."

"That would be a shame. A waste of talent."

Lorelei sat up, swung a leg over his, and then settled into his lap. "Jerk."

"Brat."

Her bottom lip stuck out in a pout. "I thought we were friends."

"We are."

"Wow. I'd hate to see how you treat your enemies, then."

"I call 'em as I see 'em."

Lorelei grabbed her shirt and pulled it over her head. Then her hands moved to the clasp of her bra and she shrugged it off her shoulders.

His hands were already moving to her waist. "And that's just beautiful."

Lorelei purred as his fingers slid over her ribs to the soft curve of her breast. Then she was pushing the buttons of his shirt through their holes. "I may be a brat, but I do have good manners. Thank you for dinner. And thanks in advance for the hot sex."

"The sex is my pleasure. The dinner was nothing."

"I know." A sexy smile tugged at her lips as she spread the two halves of his shirt open and slid her palms over his chest with a hum of appreciation. She leaned closer, her nipples barely brushing against his skin. "That's why I appreciate it."

Later, though, as Lorelei sprawled on top of him with a groan, her heartbeat thundering against his chest, Donovan wondered if it might have been something after all.

CHAPTER SEVEN

"LORELEI, COULD YOU BRING the rolls through?"

"Sure." She added a winking smiley face to Donovan's text and hit Send, then put the phone back in her purse and grabbed the bread basket. She took her seat in the same place she'd sat at for every meal at home for the last twenty-five years as Mom and Dad took their places. One day she was going to sit in Vivi's chair, just to see what the view was like from there. Maybe she'd even rearrange the furniture.

Oh, she really was a rebel. She could almost hear Donovan laughing now. She wiggled her toes inside her shoes. She'd run by the salon this morning and had them painted bright green. Then she'd had a small skull painted onto each big toe. She'd only be able to keep the design for a little while; she was planning on wearing her silver sandals to her dad's party, and green toes with skulls would *not* go over well. She'd been tempted to send Donovan a picture, but she'd rather see the look on Donovan's face when he saw them.

Which would probably not be tonight. They both had family things and lives, and they couldn't be—*shouldn't* be—in each other's pockets all the time. She tamped down the disappointment brought on by simple horniness. She would survive.

"It looks delicious, Mom." A tiny sniff set her stomach growling. Plump, perfect shrimp…the aroma of garlic and lemon wafting out of a sea of butter… Suspicion set in. Mom's scampi was her favorite, but it had fallen victim to the dietary restrictions of Dad's cardiologist. Butter—much less oceans of melted *real* butter—hadn't been in their diets for over a year now. "Is there something I should know?"

Her mother looked surprised. "What do you mean?"

"You don't eat butter anymore, so I can't help but wonder what I'm being buttered up for. You're not getting a divorce, are you?"

Dad laughed. "Of course not."

"I was just in the mood, and you being here was a perfect excuse for cheating just a little," Mom added.

"Good. I was worried there for a minute." Satisfied, she stabbed a shrimp. *Fantastic.*

"Although there *is* something we'd like to ask you. Well, something your father would like to ask you."

Dad put down his fork. Lorelei braced herself. Favorite food coupled with a serious "we'd like to ask you" didn't bode well. She braced herself before realizing that if it were really bad they'd wait until Vivi was home and tell them both at the same time. That knowledge relaxed her a small bit. "Okay. Ask away."

"My secretary wants to finalize the agenda for my retirement party—all the little details."

Dad was talking, but Mom was grinning. *Surreal.*

"I've talked Jim Nelson out of a full-fledged roast, but there will be speeches."

"Of course there will be. You've run that place for almost forty years. The speeches will probably be pleas for you not to go."

"In the interests of time," Mom interjected, "we've decided to put a limit on the number of toasts made. Your dad has narrowed the list of possibles."

"I know you'll have to let Mr. Nelson speak, but keep the microphone away from Mr. Delacroix. He rambles."

Dad nodded. "We know, Lorelei. But I've also decided I'd like a personal touch. I wanted to ask you if you'd be willing."

"To do what?"

They both laughed, adding to her confusion. Mom finally reached across the table to pat her hand.

"To make a toast for your father, darling."

She waited for the punchline. Her parents just looked at her expectantly. "Me? *Seriously?*"

"You sound surprised, dear."

Because I am completely floored by this. She gave herself a strong mental shake. "I'd be honored." At her father's smile, a warm, happy glow spread through her chest. "I promise not to roast you. Or ramble. Or get all weepy."

"Vivi said you could be counted on not to weep into the microphone."

"You asked—I mean, you've talked to Vivi?" The warm, happy glow cooled and shrank into a rather painful knot. She hadn't been Dad's first choice. She tried not to let that bother her. Much.

"She called this morning to say hi. I think she's getting a little antsy to come home. I asked her if she thought you'd like to do it, and if it would hurt her feelings if we asked you instead of her. I was afraid that you wouldn't want to do it after being 'on' so much recently."

The happy glow came racing back. *This* meant more to her than anything else. Not because she'd been asked and Vivi hadn't—it wasn't sibling rivalry—but because her parents hadn't automatically defaulted to Vivi. She'd just proved her own thesis: it was difficult, but not impossible to change people's minds. *Lorelei—one. Donovan—zip.* Oh, she couldn't wait to rub that in.

"And this is why I get shrimp scampi for dinner?" The second bite tasted even better than the first.

"It's not all about you, darling. Scampi is your dad's favorite, too."

After that dinner proceeded with the usual small talk, but mentally Lorelei was only half there. She was practically wiggling in her seat. The only thing that kept her still was years of *not* wiggling in her seat at dinner. Finally she couldn't stand it anymore and asked to be excused.

In the kitchen, she gave in to her need to do a small happy dance. She only had a minute or two before Mom would wonder why she hadn't returned, but she dug through her purse anyway. She sent a quick text to Donovan: *Can you meet me tonight around ten? Your place? I've got big news!*

She didn't have time to wait for his response, but either he could or he couldn't. She dropped her phone into her purse and went back to the table. Mom and Dad were now discussing the guest list for the party.

Her mother smiled at her a little too broadly and Lorelei braced herself. "I was thinking that you should invite Jack Morgan."

Damn. *Play dumb.* "Is he not on the list already?"

"I meant *you* should invite him. As your escort."

Dumb was not going to work. She switched to vague. "Oh…um… I don't know."

"Why not?"

"This is…" She scrambled for a good reason. "This is a family thing for us and a business thing for everyone else. I'd rather keep the focus on Dad."

"Most people there will have a plus-one. It would probably be less noticeable if you did, too," Mom countered.

"But this is a special night. I won't be able to enjoy myself if there's all that first-date pressure and jitters."

"I would think the jitters would be easier to overcome if the date itself was not the central aspect of the evening. It would take the pressure *off*."

Oh, she hated it when her mom got all reasonable like that. She felt as if she was caught in a glue trap: good and stuck but with just enough wiggle room to get stuck even worse. Dumb and vague were not going to work; she might as well face facts.

She put her fork down and leveled a look at her mother across the table. "You're not going to let this go, are you?"

Completely unrepentant, Mom shook her head. "Probably not."

"I appreciate the honesty. *But,*" she stressed as her mom started to nod, "I really don't need you setting me up on a date—much less when I know for a fact that you brainstormed this idea with Mrs. Morgan. Neither Jack nor I need a fix-up. Not with other people, and certainly not with each other."

"You said you were just waiting for Vivi to get back to town."

"I said *we*—and by *we* I meant me and Jack, not you and Mrs. Morgan—would *talk* about it after Vivi got home. It wasn't a done deal."

"I just thought this would fit the bill nicely."

Lorelei looked to her father for help, but he gave her a *you're on your own here* shrug and focused his attention closely on his plate.

"Mom, I know that you and Mrs. Mansfield are just tickled pink that Connor and Vivi ended up together after all and made you related by marriage. The whole town knows you would have betrothed them in the cradle if that had been possible. I also know that you and Mrs. Morgan are good friends, too, and you're probably thinking it would be very nice if it happened twice."

Mom didn't deny that. "It's not impossible. You and Jack might be perfect for each other."

"Maybe. But I prefer to make my own dates. Unless you think there's something wrong with me...?" she challenged.

"Of course not, honey. It's just that the pickings are starting to get rather slim."

"*Slim?* Mom, there are over a million people in the greater metro area. At least half of them have to be male. Chances are pretty good *one* of them will suit my needs."

"You know you haven't always been as choosy as you might have been with the men you've dated."

A headache began forming behind her eyes. "Oh, Lord. We're going to go *there?* Really?"

"We don't *have* to."

"Thank goodness." She speared another shrimp.

"But..."

She should have known that Mom wouldn't just drop the topic like that.

"Have you met anyone *else* you like recently?"

The shrimp got stuck in her throat. She had to grab her water glass and wash it down. *"What?"*

"You've hit every cocktail party, fund-raiser and luncheon over the past couple of weeks. I think you've met every eligible male. Maybe one of them was more to your liking."

"I was kind of busy at those events. The atmosphere wasn't exactly right for that kind of socializing." That wasn't entirely true—some people *could* do that kind of socializing at an only semi-social event. But it hadn't crossed her mind. She'd been very focused and very careful. Lord, you'd think her mom would have been *pleased* to find out she could be über-responsible and above re-proach. Of course it probably helped that she'd hooked up with Donovan right before. A memory of Julie He-bert using the guest list as a dating service flashed in her mind. *Ugh.* The thought that it could have been *her* act-ing like that…

"That doesn't mean that you couldn't have met some-one."

She could put a stop to this very easily. It was very tempting. But the knowledge of the storm that would land on her head kept her mouth firmly closed on that topic. *Gee, thinking before you speak really is a good idea.*

She leveled a look across the table. "I tried to keep it all very professional. It seems kind of inappropriate to prowl for men while at an event in a professional capacity." Her use of the word *inappropriate* was intentional. Mom had strong stands on what was appropriate and what wasn't. She laid it on a little thicker, going for Mom's most vul-nerable spots. "It never occurred to me that I should be interviewing men for dates while I was there representing Connor and the studio. Standing in for Vivi. Representing the LaBlanc family…"

Mom's lips tightened. "You've made your point, Lo-relei."

"Thank you."

"But just think about it for a day or so. That's all I ask."

She didn't have to ask what "it" was. "And if I decide in a day or so that I don't want to take Jack to the party as my date?"

"Think about it first. Keep an open mind."

She didn't have to think about it. She couldn't be less interested in Jack if he grew an extra head and started rooting for the Falcons over her beloved Saints. She was happy right now with Donovan: there was no pressure, no games, no worrying about the future. It was just easy. And fun. She was enjoying herself, enjoying having a friend, and she wanted to continue enjoying it for as long as she could. A little knot formed in her stomach at the idea that it couldn't last indefinitely and she'd have to go back to "appropriate" men her mother approved of who already had their own membership at the Club. But that was at some point in the future, and she'd worry about that once she got there.

It was all she could do to keep her face neutral as her mom finally changed the subject. Mom wanted her to keep an open mind? The openness of her mind wasn't the issue.

A family business usually meant that family dinners turned into board meetings at some point before dessert. Why, Donovan didn't quite know—it wasn't as if his father and brothers didn't see each other every day at the office, where conversations of this sort would be more appropriate. And more productive. There was a reason why small children were not normally welcome at business meals; they tended to lose interest in the conversation and devolve to surreptitiously flinging peas and kicking each other under the table.

Donovan fully admitted he was probably not helping the situation any as he thumb-wrestled with his nephew and simultaneously oversaw the construction of a mashed-potato mountain by his niece at their end of the table. He didn't have much to add to the discussion anyway, and eventually his mom would put a stop to it and insist on a different topic of conversation. So he amused himself with his nieces and nephews for the time being.

As each of his siblings had produced at least two offspring—sometimes three—every family meal bordered on chaos. It was not a place for the faint of heart or those overly concerned with proper etiquette; it was just home and family—something Donovan looked forward to mainly because it came in small doses.

His phone vibrated in his pocket as a text came in, and he pulled it out for a quick peek: *If you're going to quote me, I expect a royalty.*

Lorelei must have read today's column, where he'd addressed how hard it was to squelch rumors once they started and how damaging those rumors could be to the reputations of not only the public figures in question, but also the integrity of their legislation and legacy.

Lorelei *had* inspired the central idea: that it was difficult but not impossible to reshape people's thinking. All you had to do was prove them wrong, but that was the hard part.

Not a quote. A paraphrase. And fair use=no cash.

"Donovan's texting at the table!"

"You're supposed to be setting an example, Donovan," his mother scolded.

"Sorry, Mom." He hit Send as he put the phone back in his pocket. Then he turned to his niece and said quietly, "It's not wise to rat out an uncle who is bigger than you. *Especially* when he knows exactly how the whole 'The Paint, The Puppy and The Living Room Carpet' debacle actually went down."

Sarah, who was only seven but nobody's fool, nodded soberly. "Sorry." Eyes wide, she turned to her mother, Matt's wife Tara, and whispered, "Can I be excused now?"

"Yes, go." Tara sighed. "In fact, why don't you all go play now?"

Children bolted from the table, and the noise level in the room dropped several decibels.

Tara moved to a now-empty chair next to him and leaned back with a smile. "Ah, that's much better. By the way, she's seven. She probably doesn't know the meaning of the word *debacle*."

"She got my point, though."

"And that threat will only work until she gets old enough to figure out that I also know how it *actually* happened." Tara took a sip of her water, then grinned at him in a way that put him instantly on alert. "Speaking of things that I know—"

"That you *think* you know," he corrected. There was no way she knew the true origin of that paint.

"I was with some friends at that coffee house down from your place the other night. As we were leaving, I saw you letting a woman into your house. Normally I'd assume it was a new assistant, or the cleaning lady or something, but it was pretty late for that. And you seemed to greet her rather *un*professionally."

The rest of the St. James bloodline at the other end of the table was in animated discussion about the cost-effectiveness of longer internet spots, so there was no escape there. *Non-committal is always a safe bet.* "Hmm."

Tara leaned forward and braced her arms on the table. "Oh, come on. Who is she? It was dark, so I couldn't see her face."

"A friend."

"And does this friend have a name?"

"Of course."

"Do you *know* it?" she challenged.

"First, middle *and* last."

That earned him a frown. "But you don't want to tell me any of them?"

"Not really, no."

Tara sat back with a huff. "Anyone ever tell you that you can be a jerk sometimes?"

He wanted to laugh, but kept it in. "Now that you mention it, yes." *And a conceited blow-hard, too.*

"Are you ashamed to be seen with her or something?"

"Not at all. I just prefer keeping this private for the moment."

Tara shot a look down the table. "I won't tell your mother, if that's what you're worried about."

"Mom is quite happy with the grandchildren she has at the moment. She's not on my back to settle down and procreate anytime soon."

"Wow..." Tara managed to stretch the word into four syllables.

"What?"

"Are you implying that this is the type of woman that you'd *want* to settle down and procreate with?"

Good Lord. "I'm not implying anything. *You* are jumping way ahead."

"Well, you're not giving me much to go on. I *have* to make jumps."

"I have made a friend whose company I enjoy. She seems to enjoy mine. That's all."

Tara's eyes narrowed suspiciously. "You're not *paying* for her time and companionship, are you?"

He laughed. Lorelei would *not* like to hear she'd been accused of prostitution. "She's not a call girl, Tara. She's a friend."

"Sorry. It had to be asked."

"Why?"

"Because you normally don't have female friends. You have dates. *Rendezvous.* Affairs. Maybe the occasional fling. But a 'friend?' I'm not buying that. Anyway, if she really were *just* a friend you wouldn't be acting like this."

Tara was right—or at least partially right. How had Matt ended up with a woman that astute? "Just give me some time. See how it shapes up. If it's nothing, then there's no reason to bring anyone else into it." Tara did not look satisfied, so he threw out a promise to make her happy. "I promise that if the situation changes, you'll be one of the very first to know."

"You could just bring her to dinner soon so we can all meet her. Just as a friend. No pressure." At his look, she added primly, "Friends very often meet each other's families, you know. And a meal is quite a friendly thing."

That might not go over as well as one would hope. "I don't think Lorelei's quite ready for the full-frontal impact of a St. James family dinner."

"*Lorelei,* huh?" Tara smiled. "That's a pretty name."
Damn.

"It's unusual, too. You don't hear it all that often. I did go to school with a Lorelei years ago… Wait… No, she was a Lora Lee. Of course there's Lorelei LaBlanc—"

"More wine?" he interrupted.

Tara waved the offer away. "I'm good, thanks. I've never met her—Lorelei LaBlanc, that is—but I talked to her on the phone sometime back in the spring, when my company submitted a proposal to do the refurb on Connor Mansfield's new studio. Really nice person. But you've met her, of course. At the wed—" Tara stopped suddenly and her eyes grew wide. *"Oh…"* Once again one small word was stretched out into multiple syllables.

"What?"

Tara leaned in and dropped her voice. "Lorelei LaBlanc was the woman I saw at your house, wasn't it? I couldn't see her face, but size and hair and such all match up."

He didn't want to flat-out lie with a denial, but distraction and distortion might work. "I don't—"

"Oh. My. *God.* That reporter was right. We just all kind of laughed it off, even after she came by the offices, but…"

Thankfully no one else at the table had keyed in on their conversation yet. "Please let it go."

Tara dropped her voice to a whisper. "How long has this been going on?"

"Really, now. Do I have to beg?"

Her lips twitched. "Now that you mention it, that might be fun to watch. No wonder you're trying to keep it quiet. Her mother must be having a cow."

That would be the kindest of responses. "I don't think her family is any more aware of me than mine is—or *was* and hopefully will *continue* to be—of her."

"People are bound to find out, you know. Why the big secret?"

"Because it's nobody's business."

Tara nodded. "Fine. My lips are sealed. You like her, though, don't you?"

"I told you, she's a friend."

He was not doing a good job of selling Tara on the "friend" point. She wasn't even trying to hold back her grin. "Okay. Whatever. I just never pegged you as a social climber." She reached for her glass. "Planning on world domination now?"

He couldn't make the jump. "Excuse me?"

"I think it's called 'marrying well.' The LaBlancs are one of the oldest families in New Orleans. They have serious clout. You have money." Tara's son Jacob had toddled back into the room and skirted the table to his mother. Without even pausing, she settled him into her lap. "And you're famous already. You have some influence. But if you marry a LaBlanc you'll be simply unstoppable."

"First, I had no idea you were so Machiavellian—but you forget that I'm persona non grata in those circles, money or not."

"Why is that?"

"Between my lack of pedigree and the fact I brought down not one but two of the most powerful families in New Orleans, I'd think you'd see the problem."

Tara just waved that away. "One is not your fault and has no bearing on the kind of man you are and the other was no less than they deserved."

"Regardless, you've jumped way ahead again."

Tara grinned. "But it got you thinking, didn't it?" Tara turned to the small child tugging at her arm. "What, sweetheart?"

He whispered something behind a small, chubby hand and Tara nodded. "Excuse me." She scooped him up and sat him on her hip as she went into the next room.

Small children were quite useful as interruptions of conversations, and Donovan exhaled with relief at the reprieve. Pity Jacob hadn't had better timing. He could have saved Donovan a few uncomfortable moments.

So much for being discreet. If his sister-in-law had seen Lorelei at his house, how many other people had, too? Lorelei wasn't exactly low-profile. Half the people in the city could probably recognize her on sight; Lorelei made the papers because she was always where the cameras were. Plus, Lorelei had been in the papers a lot in the last six months or so: Vivi had become paparazzi bait the moment she'd hooked up with Connor, and Lorelei was often where they were—the Pippa to Vivi's Kate.

Honestly, he'd kind of forgotten why they were being so discreet. The one-night stand had been extended into a longer thing, but they'd stayed with the general premise of keeping their one-night stand under the radar. But why? They were both adults. It wasn't as if they had anything to hide. The local papers might have a bit of fun with another local celebrity-ish couple, but neither he nor Lorelei were nearly as high-profile as Connor and Vivi—or any of the dozen other celebrities that called New Orleans home.

His phone vibrated again. Lorelei had finally texted him back: *Who said I wanted cash? We can work it out in trade. ;-)*

That caused him to laugh. The status quo was serving him—and Lorelei, too—quite nicely at the moment. Lorelei was making the most of her time out of Vivi's shadow. She didn't need gossip or speculation on her love life becoming *another* shadow.

And him? He had no real plans for world domination—at least not plans that required Lorelei's influence for him to achieve them. He was climbing that hill quite nicely on his own. And he rather liked it that way.

Lorelei seemed okay with that, too.

Why mess with something that was working just fine?

As a kid he'd seen the LaBlanc family and others like them—the Morgans, the Mansfields and the Allisons—as golden and lucky. He'd thought that money was the only key needed for entry into that enclave, but he'd been proven wrong very quickly. His family's money had taken him from zero to hero overnight—but it hadn't brought membership into that particular circle of society. Eventually he'd convinced himself that it didn't matter and that he didn't want it. Tara's words had brought the remembrance of that feeling back.

But things were different now. He wasn't some kid just realizing his place on the food chain for the first time. He didn't care what the Morgans, the Mansfields, the Allisons or the LaBlancs thought about him. Well, except for one LaBlanc.

Lorelei was different. This situation was different. He didn't know why or how, but it was. And while it probably would never be more than just this, he was fine with that.

Tara kept giving him knowing looks the rest of the evening, and he'd swear at one point his other sister-in-law, Mary, was giving him one, too. He hoped it was paranoia and not that Tara was sharing her new-found information.

His phone vibrated again.

Can you meet me tonight around ten? Your place? I've got big news!

When Lorelei had left last night she'd said she probably wouldn't be able to see him tonight as she needed to put in some quality time with her parents. Whatever this big news was, she was obviously excited about it. He glanced at the time and texted her back that he would.

When Matt asked if he wanted to do a brotherly night out to a local club where a friend of theirs was playing, Donovan claimed he had an early meeting the next day. He caught Tara's smirk out of the corner of his eye.

Tara was probably right. If he and Lorelei kept this up eventually someone would see them. It would get out.

And Lorelei's mother would not be the only person in New Orleans to have a cow when *that* happened.

Lorelei navigated the tiny alley behind Donovan's house and pulled in behind his car. She was late, but she just hadn't been able to escape her mother gracefully, having to finally resort to a claim of a headache in order to get out of there. She must be getting better at lying, though, because her mother hadn't batted an eyelash about it.

She rang the bell, but instead of releasing the lock, Donovan spoke over the intercom. "Can I help you?"

"It's me."

"You're late, you know."

Cheeky thing. "If you check your phone," she said carefully, "you'll see that I at least sent you a text letting you know."

A second later the lock on the gate was released. Donovan was waiting for her by the French doors.

"You big jerk."

"Couldn't resist."

Lorelei shook her head. He was just too cute to stay peevish at, and she was just a sucker. When he stepped back to let her in she noticed that there was a champagne bucket and two glasses on the coffee table. "Wow."

"Well, you said it was big news. I figured we might need it."

"You're so sweet."

"I thought I was a big jerk?"

"You're that, too."

Donovan popped the cork and poured two glasses. "Whatever it is, congratulations," he toasted. After she drank, he motioned her to the couch. "So, what's the big news?"

"You know my dad is retiring, right?" She waited for him to nod. "His partners and some other folks he's done business with over the years are throwing him this huge retirement bash. They've been working on the plans for like a month. So, tonight Mom and Dad tell me that they need to get the agenda finalized and, long story short, Dad asks me to make a toast."

"That's great. Congratulations."

Her grin felt as if it was about to split her face. "Thanks. I mean, I've had so many great things happen recently— new opportunities opening up and all—but this… This is actually probably the best thing of all. There are so many people that he could have asked, but he asked *me*. Me! Can you believe that?"

"Actually, I can. I've seen you in action, remember?"

Donovan seemed totally sincere, and that meant more to her than she'd expected.

"I don't know why you're *so* surprised, though. You made a toast at the wedding."

"Yes, but that was Vivi's choice. *I* was under very strict supervision by my mother the whole time." She rolled her eyes at the memory. "Not only did Mom oversee the writing of it, but I'd been threatened to within an inch of my life if I mucked it up. That toast was the first sip of alcohol that crossed my lips that night."

He waggled his eyebrows at her. "You certainly made up for it later."

"Very funny."

"Is your mom going to supervise this one, as well?"

"Believe it or not, I don't think so. It seems I've proven myself now and don't need maternal speechwriting tips anymore."

"And you haven't been threatened within an inch of your life either, I take it?"

"Amazingly, no. Six months of good behavior was all it took."

"Six months? I thought this was all just while Vivi was out of town."

"God, no." She sighed. "*That* would have been *so* much easier. But as you quoted me—"

"Paraphrased you," he corrected.

She raised an eyebrow but said nothing. "It's not been an easy task to get to this point. I had to lay the groundwork first. Go low-profile, behave myself, show proper atonement for the sins of my youth. If I hadn't done that, then I wouldn't have been able to 'prove myself' these past few weeks."

"I had no idea you'd put so much thought into this plan." Understanding crossed his face. "No wonder you were so worried about that mention in the paper. Or getting caught leaving my hotel room."

"Exactly."

He lifted his glass again. "Well, it seems you formed a worthy plan and that it worked out exactly like you hoped. Cheers."

"I'll drink to that."

Donovan refilled her glass. "Now that you've accomplished those parts of the plan, what's next?"

"Do I have plans for world domination, you mean? Plans to stage a coup and steal Vivi's place as the saint of New Orleans?" She leaned back against the cushions and got comfortable.

"Something like that."

She shook her head. "I don't want Vivi's life. I now know that for a fact. All that love comes with a price tag I'm not willing to pay. I'll never be a pillar of society, but that's not really me anyway."

He sat at the other end. "I agree."

"I'm not sure that's a compliment."

"I'd be very disappointed to see you end up exactly like your mother."

Lorelei pushed herself up. "Hey, careful now..."

"It's not an insult against your mother, so there's no need to get your back up."

Temporarily mollified, she let him continue.

"I just don't see you as the matron and patron of social and civic clubs who lunches more than anything else."

That gave her pause. "You know, I don't see me there either—although I think my mother is already ordering me white gloves and filling out my paperwork for junior membership in the Ladies' Auxiliary Guild as we speak. I just have to find the happy medium before it gets out of hand."

Donovan looked surprised. "Do you not *want* to be in the Ladies' Auxiliary Guild?

"Not really."

"Isn't that some kind of status symbol, though?"

"Yes, but they don't *really* do anything other than lunch. They used to, but it's kind of lost its focus. I think I'd rather spend my time a bit more productively." She hadn't really thought it through before, so the realization was new to her, too. "There are so many worthy causes where I could really make a difference. I need to use my time effectively to make the most impact and do the most good." The look on Donovan's face had her laughing. "Yes, I know. It's a bit surprising to me, too. Look at me—I'm growing as a person. I'm no Vivi, but I'm rather liking this Lorelei."

"I rather like Lorelei, too," he said with a quiet laugh.

Her heart flopped over in her chest at his words, and the air felt really heavy all of a sudden. The silence was deafening as *something* shifted between them.

Then Donovan cleared his throat. "Uh…more champagne?"

"Yes! Please." She still had almost half a glass, and she stuck it out so fast the contents sloshed over the rim. Donovan reached for her hand and slowly licked the drops of liquid away. The feel of his tongue on her skin brought a different and far more familiar tension into the air, and Lorelei grabbed the shift in mood gratefully. Donovan looked up and that sexy grin sent little tingles all over her skin in anticipation.

"This gives me ideas."

"I think I'm quite interested in these ideas."

With a leer, Donovan pulled her to her feet and grabbed the champagne bucket off the table. She followed him quickly up the stairs, glad to leave whatever that disturbing moment was behind.

CHAPTER EIGHT

ON DAYS LIKE TODAY even the locals were allowed to complain about the weather. The heat hit Lorelei like a wall the minute she stepped onto her porch, and the humidity was so high she could almost see the moisture in the air.

Today was the kind of day that should be spent sitting very still with a cold drink, but of course today was the day she had a million things to do. Post office, bank, drop off paychecks at the studio and the art gallery...all the minutiae of her life. Thankfully Vivi would be home the day after tomorrow and would take back her own errands and minutiae.

A frantic, panicked search for her iPad hadn't exactly gotten her day off to a great start, but she'd called Donovan—waking him up—and he'd found it under the couch, where it had slid out of her bag. Although he'd grumbled about it, he had agreed to meet her to return it.

After listening to the weather report this morning she'd skipped make-up altogether—it wouldn't have stayed on anyway—and pulled her hair up into a clip off her neck. She was wearing as little clothing as decency and good taste allowed, but sweat still rolled down her spine as she crossed one errand after the other off her list. Now she was running a little late to meet Donovan, but *actually* running was out of the question. Not in this heat. She had too much to do today to take time out for heatstroke.

Red-faced, sunburned, equally sweaty tourists meandered in the streets, going into shops primarily for the air-conditioning. Lorelei resisted that urge, since she only had two blocks to go, but she opened the door to the little coffee shop on Magazine Street gratefully and stood there for a moment enjoying the cool air.

Donovan was at a table over in the corner, reading something on his phone. He, too, was dressed in deference to the weather, and Lorelei fought back a grin. He looked much younger and not at all serious and punditlike in a grey T-shirt, khaki shorts and running shoes. *Wow, great calves.* How had she not noticed that before?

He was unshaven, hair slightly mussed, managing to hit that sweet spot between adorable and yummy perfectly. He looked up as she approached, and his smile tipped the scale in favor of yummy.

"Hey," he said, putting away his phone. "You look…" his lips twitched "…really hot."

"Hush. It's the armpit of hell out there." She dropped her bag on the chair and caught the server's eye.

"Yes, it is. Tell me again why I had to come out in it?"

"Because I still have to go to Vivi's to water the plants and drop off paychecks at the studio and then go back out to Mom's. I wasn't about to go all the way to your place, too." When the server came around, she ordered a large iced tea and got settled into the seat across from Donovan.

"Aw, so you just wanted to see me? How sweet."

He said it teasingly, but it hit a chord inside her. She *did* miss seeing him. But, looking at the smirk on his face, she knew she'd be able to ice skate on the sidewalk out front before she'd admit it. "I'm organized. This is a natural breaking point to my errands today."

"Why do you have to go back out to your parents'?" His eyebrows drew together in concern. "Is everything okay?"

The show of concern touched her. "Just party stuff. That's why I need my iPad."

He slid it across the table with a grin. "Maybe you're not so organized after all."

"Well, if you hadn't distracted me last night I might not have—"

"Lorelei?"

She turned, looking for the voice, and froze. *Awkward.* "Cynthia. Wow, this is a surprise." She finally got herself moving to stand and accept Cynthia's hug. "I haven't seen you in ages." When Cynthia's father had gone to jail, most of their assets had been seized, and the DuBois family had been forced to move to Chalmette. Shamed, they'd all but disappeared.

Cynthia's voice was cold and stilted. "This *is* a surprise." She looked pointedly at Donovan. "Quite a big one."

Oh, yeah, *really* awkward. *What to do?* Good manners said one thing; common sense said something else entirely. But since Cynthia didn't seem willing just to move on and let this pass without comment, she fell back on good manners to try to control it. "Cyn, I don't know if you've ever actually *met* Donovan St. James before?"

"No, I haven't." Each excruciatingly polite word could cut glass. Lorelei was giving Cynthia the opportunity to walk away, but Cynthia wasn't taking it. "Please do introduce us."

Donovan shot her a questioning look as he stood, obviously aware that there was something going on, but still acting as if this would be a somewhat normal introduction. "Awkward" quickly morphed into "downright uncomfortable."

"Donovan, this is Cynthia DuBois." Donovan didn't seem to make the connection, but DuBois was a common enough name. "Lincoln DuBois's daughter," she clarified.

The name dropped like a gauntlet. Donovan finally twigged to the problem and the hand he'd begun to extend fell back to his side. "I see. I'd say nice to meet you, but I, too, will go with this is a surprise."

Cynthia shot Donovan a look of pure hate, then dismissed him rudely, pulling Lorelei a few feet away and turning her back on him completely. "What the sweet hell are you doing with Donovan St. James?"

"Well...I..."

"Good God, Lorelei. Have you lost your mind?"

"No, I—"

Cynthia wasn't waiting for explanations. Her head might explode if she didn't calm down. "After what he *did,* you and he are—?"

Oh, God, this was going to be ugly. Lorelei lowered her voice in the hope Cynthia would do the same. "Cyn, calm down."

"I will *not* calm down. He destroyed my family, my *life.*"

Even Lorelei knew that Lincoln DuBois and his cronies were completely responsible for their own destruction; the fallout on their families was also their own fault. But she understood the feelings of Cynthia and the others, too. And, if she was honest with herself, a few weeks ago she'd *shared* them.

"Do your parents know about this?"

Ice slid down her spine. "What?"

"That you're all chummy with him? Are you dating him or something?"

Cynthia was practically shouting, and they now had the attention of everyone in the shop. Thankfully it wasn't that many people, but an audience only made this worse. "Cyn, it's not worth the outrage."

"Then what are you doing, exactly?"

"Donovan is…" She couldn't bring herself to look in his direction as she searched for an excuse. "Donovan is a major donor to one of Connor's projects. I'm Connor's assistant, remember?"

"So this is a business meeting?"

"Yes, business." Lorelei was surprised at how easily the lie came off her tongue. Self-preservation had obviously improved her acting ability.

Her eyes narrowed. "Here? Dressed like *that?*"

Cynthia had at least one good point. Not only was she not dressed particularly businesslike—even for the lackadaisical dress code of the music business—the powerful air-conditioning had cooled her enough that her nipples were now showing through her shirt. She certainly didn't look very professional.

"Cyn—"

"Well, don't let me interrupt your 'meeting.' Just make sure you get as much money out of him as you can. Since he made quite a bit of it from destroying my family, consider it a donation from me, as well. At least his ill-gotten gains will serve some good."

Cynthia needed a reality check, but this was neither the time nor the place. Her family's money was the ill-gotten gains; Donovan had just been the one to call them on it.

Their server, who must have somehow missed hearing Cynthia's tirade, returned with Lorelei's drink and set it on the table. Then she turned to Cynthia and asked innocently, "Will you be joining them?"

Cynthia's laugh was sharp and brittle. "Not even if you paid me."

"Oh…um…okay, then." The server looked around uncomfortably, and Lorelei mentally doubled the poor girl's tip. Finally she asked, "Well, can I get you anything?"

"No, I'm leaving."

The server scurried away, relief written on her face, and Cynthia turned back to Lorelei, anger and disappointment etched equally across her face.

"Lorelei, I just don't know what to say."

Desperate to smooth things, Lorelei said the first thing that came to mind. "Call me soon, okay? We'll go to lunch."

Cynthia gave her the tiniest of nods. Then, turning to Donovan, Cynthia twisted her mouth into a snarl. "You can just go to hell." On that note, she picked up Lorelei's tea and dumped it into Donovan's lap. Then she stormed out.

"Oh, my God." Lorelei called over to the server to bring towels as Donovan picked the ice cubes out of his lap. "Sorry about that."

Donovan waved away the apology. "I guess I should be glad you ordered iced tea and not hot. I just hope it wasn't sweet tea. I'd hate to be wet *and* sticky."

Relieved Donovan wasn't going to be angry, Lorelei took the towels from the server—whose tip had just been quadrupled—and tried to help clean up. "I think that's what they call a classic case of misplaced anger."

"I've heard worse." He held up a hand. "I've got this, Lorelei." After using the towels to mop up the worst of it, Donovan left cash on the table and headed toward the door. Lorelei added another twenty to the pile as an apology to the server and followed him.

"Did you drive?" When he shook his head, she said, "Neither did I. It's a long walk in wet pants, though. Want to see if we can find a cab?"

"It's fine. In a few minutes I'm sure the wet fabric will feel refreshing in this heat. I'll talk to you later."

"Wait, I'll go with you."

Donovan might not be angry, per se, but he certainly wasn't finding this funny, either. "Not necessary. Go finish your errands."

Something was *very* wrong. "Okay. I'll see you tonight?"

Donovan merely nodded.

She watched him leave. That had not gone well. She never would have thought Cynthia DuBois the type to make a big public scene like that. Obviously the last few years had changed her and made her bitter.

Lorelei was feeling a little bitter herself. In her anger at Donovan, Cynthia had ruined Lorelei's day, as well. *What a spoiled brat.*

And, while it wasn't her fault, Lorelei still felt as if she owed Donovan an apology.

He should have recognized Cynthia DuBois—she'd stared him down the entire time he'd been on the witness stand at the trial that had sent her father to jail—but the intervening years hadn't been kind to her. The DuBois family had not been sent into poverty, but they'd lost most of their money, and without that, Cynthia had lost her expensive shine.

He had to give her credit; her honest reaction was a nice change from the cold shoulders and avoidance by the other families involved and their friends. While it hadn't been personal—at least not for him—he wasn't stupid or naive enough to believe that she hadn't taken it personally. Honestly, he should be glad Cynthia had only dumped a drink into his lap. Lanelle DuBois, Cynthia's mother, had slapped him in front of a full press conference, in addition to questioning his ethics, his intelligence, his heritage and his legitimacy. At least Cynthia had restrained herself more than her mother had.

But neither Cynthia's insults nor his wet pants were what was bothering him hours after the fact. It was Lorelei.

The look that had crossed her face when she'd heard her name…

He couldn't quite describe it. The closest he'd come was an adolescent "oh-God-I'm-so-busted" look—one that encompassed guilt and shame and worry about repercussions.

And it had crossed her face *before* she'd turned—*before* she'd seen that it was Cynthia DuBois.

The only explanation was that she'd considered herself "busted" no matter *who* it had been.

Even worse, though, was the echo of it he'd seen when Cynthia had asked if her parents "knew."

If he hadn't known already, that look would have answered the question with a big fat "no." The fact that Lorelei didn't want her social life overshadowing her attempts at redemption in Vivi's absence was a fair enough reason to keep their association quiet, but that had been *horror* at the thought of her parents finding out.

He pulled a beer from the fridge and leaned against the counter, not sure what to make of today's events. He wasn't happy, but he couldn't put his finger on exactly why…

The bell on the back gate chimed, announcing Lorelei's arrival, and he reached for the button to release the lock. A minute later Lorelei was at the French doors.

She was still in the tank top and shorts she'd worn earlier, and carried a leather bag strapped across her chest.

"Hey." She rose up on tiptoes to for a quick kiss. "Careful—I'm all sweaty."

"Did you walk here?"

"Of course I walked. I try not to drive in the Quarter unless I have to—much less on a Saturday night. It's too easy to get frustrated and decide to take out a pedestrian or two." She removed the bag and set it on the counter, flashing a cheeky smile. "I figured if I got too sweaty you wouldn't object to a shower." She motioned to his beer. "Can I have one of those?"

He got another one, and she took a long swallow before digging into her bag and producing a small blue gift bag tied with a white ribbon. She handed it over almost shyly.

"What's this?"

"A present, silly. Open it."

He did, to find a generic CD with *Monty Jones/Connor Mansfield* and a date written in her handwriting across the front. He looked at her in confusion.

"I saw you had some Monty Jones in your collection, and he was at the studio about a month ago, jamming with Connor. I made a few phone calls this afternoon and got the okay to burn you a disk. It was a casual thing for them, and none of it has been through post-production, but it's pretty good."

It was a personal and thoughtful gift. He was oddly touched. "Thanks, Lorelei."

He could tell she'd been worried when she broke into a smile. "Well, you didn't seem like a flowers kind of guy and I needed an opening salvo."

"For an apology?"

"Yeah, because I owe you one this time. This afternoon was just...*bad*. I'm sorry. I really should have handled that better. It caught me off-guard, though."

Maybe he'd been overthinking it. Looking for insult when none was intended. He'd never done that before. But this was Lorelei, and it seemed he was a little touchy on that subject. "Me, too."

"So you're not mad at me?"

"You're not the one who dumped a drink on me."

"I know, but…" She sighed. "As you said, at least it was cold. Although I imagine that's not very nice, either."

She moved her eyes toward his zipper, and his body reacted even if his mind was still at odds.

She chuckled. "I was about to ask if you were fully recovered, but I think I have my answer." She winked at him. "I've got to admit, though, you handled that much better than I would have."

"Really?"

"Oh, yeah." Lorelei boosted herself up onto the counter. "I'd have probably totally freaked and there would have been hair-pulling and cat-scratching and a trip to the police station involved."

Tough talk, but he couldn't imagine Lorelei doing any such thing. He doubted the LaBlanc women ever got physical in an argument. It wouldn't be very ladylike. But he nodded anyway. "Thereby totally destroying that image you've been so carefully crafting?"

"Oh, definitely. That's why I'm glad it was you and not me. Can you see me trying to explain to my parents that I got arrested?"

"I'd have bailed you out."

"I appreciate the sentiment, but that might have only made it worse." She laughed. "Oh, I can see me explaining *that*."

Maybe it was just the fact that the look on Lorelei's face earlier was still fresh in his mind, but this conversation was making warning bells clang in his head. "Me bailing you out would be worse than you getting arrested?"

"Hmm, that's a hard one. Don't know." She laughed again. "I don't really want to find out, either."

Okay, he really didn't like this conversation. And he didn't like the fact he didn't like this conversation, either. "An arrest record might keep you out of the Junior Ladies' Whatever."

"I hadn't thought of it that way... The idea holds merit. I'll keep it in mind for the future. Actually, it might solve several problems. How does one go about getting arrested?"

"I've never been arrested, but I assume one breaks the law." He took another drink, and when Lorelei stayed silent he asked, "What problems?"

"Excuse me?"

"You said there were several problems an arrest would solve. I'm wondering exactly what those might be."

Lorelei's sigh held resignation and frustration, with a bit of exasperated humor, as well. "Just my mother's general insanity."

"Worse than white gloves and the Junior Ladies' Whatever?"

She seemed to weigh that. "Maybe. But it's nothing I can't handle. Did you do anything interesting this afternoon?"

"Okay, now I'm *really* curious."

Her mouth twisted. "Jack Morgan asked me out. Did you know that?"

That need to punch Jack in the mouth came roaring back. "It was rather obvious he was gearing up for it. What did you tell him?"

"That I was really superbusy right now and totally booked until Vivi gets back to town."

That wasn't exactly the flat denial he'd have liked to

hear. "So now that Vivi's return is imminent he's ready to take you at your word?"

"Obviously Jack is not familiar with the polite brush-off."

That mollified him a little. But only a little. "Most men are completely blind and deaf in that area of social inter-action. You have to be direct." There were several direct and obvious ways for Lorelei to respond to Jack's offer, but they hadn't seemed to occur to her. Why?

"I can't. Not now."

"Because…?"

Another eye roll from Lorelei. "Because now my mom and his mom have this great plan of breeding us or some-thing. Let's just say it's a good thing I can't be married off without my permission in this century."

"You're exaggerating."

"Not by much." She took another drink and sighed. "It's the only thing putting a damper on my anticipation of Dad's party."

"Not following you."

"Oh, did I skip that part? Mom has this really great idea that I should ask Jack to be my date for Dad's party."

"What did she say when you told her no?"

"I didn't exactly say that," she hedged.

He didn't like where this was going. "You told her you *would?*"

"No. She's knows I'm not keen on the idea, and we left it at 'I'll think about it.'"

He must have looked at her funny because Lorelei went on the defensive.

"It was in the middle of dinner. I was trapped. I couldn't think of a more graceful way out."

"You tell her you don't need to be fixed up on a date."

"I tried that, but without a really good reason to back

it up it rings a little hollow. She can't understand why I'd rather go stag and mess up the seating chart than go with eligible and good-catch Jack Morgan."

He simply could not hold his suspicions at bay any longer. He'd ignored the alarm bells as long as he could. Casually, belying the acidic taste in his mouth, he offered, "I could be your date for the evening."

Lorelei stilled, her beer halfway to her mouth, and shot him an *Are you insane?* look. "After what happened today with Cynthia DuBois, do you really think that's a good idea? People are still very touchy about that issue. And the ones who are the touchiest are on the guest list already."

"I can handle it." The question was, could *she?* Donovan was pretty sure he knew the answer to that.

"That's very brave of you, but party-etiquette rule number one prohibits me from intentionally inciting a riot among the guests. When possible, it's best to make sure that the presence of one guest won't cause embarrassment or distress for the other guests."

"Including you?" he challenged.

Confusion wrinkled her brow. "A riot would certainly distress me. It's my father's party and I don't want anything to ruin that."

At that, Donovan was done with this game. "Like his precious daughter showing up with Donovan St. James?"

Guilt streaked across her face so fast he nearly missed it. "I don't know what you mean."

"Don't play dumb. It's beneath you—and insulting to us both. There's a real easy way out of your mom's matchmaking. You tell her you're seeing me."

She shook her head. "It wouldn't matter. Here's a newsflash—my mom's not real crazy about you. She'd still try to match me up with Jack."

"And you can't be seen with someone your parents wouldn't approve of?"

He waited for a denial. It didn't come and he wasn't surprised.

"It's complicated, Donovan."

Strangely, he was disappointed that he wasn't surprised. But he was more disappointed than he liked to admit at her words. He stood. "Not really. The simple fact is that you don't want *anyone* to know you've been sleeping with me."

"Of course I don't."

That cut deeper than he'd expected. "At least now you're being honest."

He recognized the set of her jaw.

"I don't want *anyone* to know who I'm sleeping with because my sex life is none of anyone else's business. It's not something I feel I have to advertize."

"You're ashamed of yourself."

She sat up straight. "What?"

"Not of what you're doing, but *who* you're doing it with. At a certain point people who are seen in each other's company often enough are generally assumed to be sleeping together, as well. So it's not *what* people will think about what you're doing that you're worried about. It's the fact they'll know you're doing it with *me.* You're ashamed to be seen with *me.*"

She shook her head. "That's not true. Not entirely true," she corrected. "There's a lot more going on."

He didn't really care. He just wanted to cut to the facts. "Why'd you tell Cynthia DuBois that we were having a business meeting today?"

"To protect her feelings. Her reasons may not be completely valid, but I understand why she feels the way she does. And she considers me a friend, so I was trying to make her feel a little better. I didn't realize your ego was so damn fragile."

He wasn't going to take that bait. "This isn't about my ego. It's about yours. The easiest way out of a date with Jack is to show up with me. But you can't do that because then everyone will know you've gone slumming."

Lorelei's jaw dropped but she didn't say anything, telling him with her silence that he'd hit the target with that jab.

"At least it's safe slumming," he continued. "I've got my own money and my own connections, so it's not like you're sleeping with a bartender or pool boy or someone *really* beneath you. You're not brave enough to date someone just to spite your family and your friends because you desperately want their approval."

At that, Lorelei's mouth slammed shut and her lips pressed into a thin line. Oh, yeah, he was definitely on target. He wished he'd had this insight weeks ago. He'd just been too caught up in Lorelei's spell to see the obvious. For someone who made his living going past the obvious, digging into the layers and finding out the truth… Well, it was a little humbling to find out he'd been so blind. He blamed the humbling and the disappointment for the feeling in his chest, since he didn't know how to describe it otherwise. He didn't like it, though.

"So you've gotten to do your little rebellion—sneaking around, banging the one guy guaranteed to horrify everyone you know and getting your kicks because you're getting away with it. Well, I'm done playing. You know the way out." He tossed the bottle toward the bin and walked away, leaving her sitting there on the counter before he said something he'd really regret.

"What the hell, Donovan?" She actually looked shocked and confused.

"I'm not interested in being your dirty little secret, Princess."

Her mouth snapped closed.

A dirty little secret. He'd been made brutally aware of the concept in high school. And he really resented the fact that Lorelei had him—a fully grown, successful adult—reliving high-school dramas.

Penny Richards. Daughter of a city councilman and cocaptain of the cheerleading squad. She'd cornered him under the bleachers after homecoming his junior year, and they'd snuck around for months like something out of a teenage movie. After a year of being only slightly better off than an outcast—he'd been good at sports, so he hadn't been completely ignored, but he hadn't been "one of them," either—it had been almost romantic, the two of them from different worlds. Hell, he'd been young, and just happy to be getting laid at all, so he hadn't really questioned it.

Then the news that his family's company had hit the Forbes list had spread through New Orleans like water from a broken levee. Figuring he was about to break through some invisible wall, he'd asked Penny to prom—only to be turned down flat and unceremoniously dumped.

All because she was too good for some "tacky *nouveau riche* social-climber." It was the first time he'd heard the term, and he'd had to look it up. With that knowledge, his entire understanding of the world had shifted. Nothing would change the fact he wasn't one of them. That invisible wall could not be broken through, and nor could it be climbed. It was actually better to be poor than nouveau riche.

It had been a hard-learned lesson, and one he'd been sure he would never forget.

Of course now it seemed he *had* forgotten that lesson,

or else he'd have steered far and wide of Lorelei LaBlanc. And he probably would have except for large amounts of alcohol. The ramifications of that had shown him a bit of Lorelei he hadn't expected.

And he'd lost sight of the obvious.

CHAPTER NINE

It took a second for Donovan's words to register fully, and by then he was out of the room. Lorelei had been wavering between anger and shame and guilt, but "Princess" took her straight into anger.

She hopped down off the counter and followed him into the living room. "You don't get to throw a grenade like that and then walk away."

"I just did, Lorelei. I'm done talking."

A red haze clouded her vision and she forced herself not to yell. "Well, I'm not. You know, you're not wrong—but you're pretty damn far from right, too. *Yes,* I'm sneaking around, sleeping with a guy simply because the sex is good. *No,* my family and my friends would not approve of that. *Yes,* their approval is very important to me. I'm really freakin' sorry that you don't see that."

"Oh, I see it. I just think you're shallow for caring that much."

"Shallow?" Oh, now she wanted to hit something. Namely him. "Wanting to spare the feelings of the people I love and respect makes me shallow? Showing respect for the society I was raised in, the traditions and the culture and the values that I was taught makes me *shallow?"*

"I'm well aware of the 'traditions and the culture' and

the so-called 'values' you were taught. They *are* pretty damn shallow."

"And you know this how, exactly?"

"Because they are. And the truth is *you* don't actually think they're important enough to really care about, either—you just want people to *think* you care."

Something about that nagged at her. "I'm trying to build something here, trying to make something out of my life, and that's not been easy."

"Making something out of your life is an admirable thing."

Finally. "Then why are you giving me grief over it?

"As I said, because you're more worried about what people think of you than what you actually are."

That nasty tone had her digging her nails into her palms as she forced her hands to stay at her sides. "So I should be like you and not give a damn at all what people think?"

Donovan shot her a look. "It works."

She shot him one back. "Not as well as you think."

"What the hell does that mean?"

"Being involved with you will horrify everyone I know. But it's not because I'm 'slumming,' as you so tactlessly put it. I could bang the pool boy if I wanted to, and while everyone would *tsk* and shake their heads they'd get over it. It would just show poor judgment on my part, but that's not a crime. The problem is you. Specifically. Not your family or your finances. *You.* You're so damn smug. If anyone thinks they're better than somebody else, it's you."

"You're the one riding on the LaBlanc name."

"And your name is sitting like a chip on your shoulder. You've figured out that your money can't buy you class and respectability in some people's eyes, so you just mock what you can't have."

Donovan's eyes narrowed. She might be on to something here. Julie's speech about "marrying up" came rushing back to her.

"That's what bugs you about this, isn't it? Even if you bag one of the LaBlanc girls, you still can't get into the country club. Is that the problem? That even if I were willing to let you try, you couldn't ride on my name for your gain? Feeling a bit resentful, are we?"

There was a tiny twitch that might have been guilt, but his voice was cold and sarcastic. "Join the rest of us in twenty-first century America, Lorelei. You aren't some kind of European aristocrat."

"Then don't pretend that your 'humble' roots make you some kind of hero with an all-American success story, either. Let me remind you that you got your start on your daddy's money, too."

Donovan's jaw tightened. "I've made quite a bit on my own. Built my own reputation. Can't say the same for you, though."

"You know, you're right. I've realized recently that I still have a lot of work to do. I've got a lot to live up to. But I've got my own plans, too. I've been tying myself in knots over you, but for all the wrong reasons. You're not the right kind of guy, but it's not why you think."

She turned her back on him with every intention of leaving before this got any uglier—not that she could see how it could sink any lower.

"And you're an expert on what I think now?"

It was a cold drawl—one she recognized from years past as well as from his TV interviews as the warning note that Donovan was about to rip someone to shreds.

But she wasn't really worried. "I'm getting there. You've decided that I'm an elitist snob. A princess who thinks she's too good for the likes of you. And you're right. I *am* too good to waste my time with someone who disdains everything about me and everything I care about. My shame is that I thought it mattered."

She stomped into the kitchen, grabbed her bag and exited through the door she'd entered just a little while earlier with such excitement. She let her anger carry her a full block before she leaned against a building to gather herself.

Where did Donovan get off with that holier-than-thou attitude? Slumming, indeed. If anyone thought they were slumming, it was Donovan. She was glad to be proved right—at least in her desire to keep things between them on the down-low. Any guilt she'd felt about keeping him her "dirty little secret" was quickly being assuaged. Honestly, if she'd dealt with the fallout of seeing him and then realized how deep his disdain for her went... *That* would have been humiliating.

Oh, to turn back the calendar three weeks and fight that curiosity that had led her into Donovan's bed a second time. She hadn't done well in chemistry in high school—and she'd failed it miserably this time.

At least no one knew. There would be no awkward questions, no shaking of heads or I-told-you-sos. She'd had a fling. It was done now, and she'd go back to her regularly scheduled life.

Why did it hurt? She didn't know what was worse: the fact he'd said those things, or the fact he believed them. No, the fact that she cared that he'd said them was the worst.

Sighing, she pushed off the wall and started the trek home. The streets of the Quarter were busier now. With the sun down, the bars and clubs were gearing up. Sunburned tourists in T-shirts were now about equally balanced by the club crowd: the young and beautiful and dressed up, out to enjoy themselves.

Not long ago she probably would have been one of them. There was a small sigh of regret for what she'd given up. Suddenly she felt very old for twenty-five.

It wasn't as if she couldn't have that life back. She could be one of the local socialites—it wasn't as if there wasn't acceptance for that. Expectations were very low, but as long as her behavior stayed within legal boundaries and a certain level of decorum she could easily go back. While her parents would be disappointed, they wouldn't disown her or anything.

At the same time she was very proud of what she'd accomplished and didn't want to give that up. She was rather liking the fact that people wanted to talk to her about more than superficial things. That they cared about her opinion and wanted her as a representative for their mission. Her whole life she'd been accepted because she was someone's daughter, granddaughter or, more recently, sister. It was nice actually to have her own name, her own place, her own slice of respect that didn't come only because she was a LaBlanc.

If Donovan couldn't understand that...

And *had* he been hoping that he'd benefit through their association? She'd seen that quick flash. Maybe he'd been planning on making connections through *her* connections. He had his own money and influence, and his friendship with Connor and Vivi had him traveling in new circles. Had he hoped to expand those circles? Was that why he'd suddenly changed his tune when she showed interest?

She now understood one of the mantras she'd heard her whole life. When you dated inside your own circle you didn't have to worry about things like that. It was why like married like. Julie had just put it a bit more bluntly. It had as much to do with self-preservation as anything else. She wouldn't have these questions if she'd just remembered that one simple fact that had been pounded into her psyche her entire life.

She'd chalk this up as a learning experience. She'd know better next time.

It wasn't anything. She'd known that going in.

Then why did it hurt?

Lorelei stroked the silk sarong almost reverently. She'd never felt anything quite as luxurious in her life. "It's beautiful, Vivi. Thanks."

"I've got a necklace for you in here somewhere that matches it nicely..." Vivi frowned at the luggage exploding over the bed.

Even after a ridiculously long flight from the Seychelles, when any normal person would look like hell on toast from jet lag and dehydration, Vivi looked perfect. As always. In fact she looked rested and refreshed, her skin lightly tanned and highlights from the sun in her hair. Lorelei had always questioned the wisdom of highlights since her hair was so dark, but they certainly looked good on Vivi. Maybe she'd reconsider.

Both Connor and Vivi had tons to catch up on—she knew this for a fact since she'd been holding down the fort while they lounged on a beach—and Connor had headed straight for the studio this morning. But she and Vivi had gone to brunch instead, and Lorelei was now curled up on the chaise in Vivi's bedroom, scrolling through their pictures while Vivi made her jealous with details from her vacation.

"It all sounds amazing. And the beach looks gorgeous. I'm *so* ready to go someplace other than here. It's been nasty hot for weeks and, honestly, your life is not that much fun."

"I'm glad to hear you think that, because I'm ready to

take it back. Being away from it all was nice for about a week. Then I started to get bored."

"Only you."

"But I hear you've done quite well in my place."

"You've been home for twelve hours. How could you possibly know that?"

Vivi looked downright smug. "Just because you ignore my emails, don't assume others do."

"You were on your honeymoon. You're not supposed to email people while you're on your honeymoon. You're supposed to relax and have fun."

"I did. But now I'm done. Do we need to go over anything to bring me up to speed?"

Lorelei shook her head. "I typed up notes from everything—all the people I talked to, what you need to follow up on—and emailed the files to you this morning. Just let me know if you have any questions." She sighed and leaned back. She felt as if she'd just passed on a very heavy mantle, and the relief felt divine.

She'd done the same gathering and organizing for Connor, but that was her job. Connor was probably in his office right now, going through those files and making more work for her to do. And she looked forward to it, because she did love what she did, but Vivi's stuff...that wasn't hers. She'd been wearing borrowed shoes for almost a month, and it felt good to be back in her own.

"Those are some pretty deep sighs. Everything okay?"

"Yeah. Just tired. Oh, and now that you're back *you* can deal with Mom. She's wigging over Dad's party, and she's not even the hostess."

"I'll sort her out. We're meeting them for dinner tonight." There was that smug look again. "Want me to start with the Jack Morgan situation?"

Unbelievable. "How do you know there's a situation?"

"I told you—other people respond to my emails. Mom's right, though. Jack's a good catch. And he's a nice guy."

Lorelei just hummed a non-committal response.

"But I also agree with you that Dad's party is not the best time or place for a first date."

"Thank you. At least someone agrees with me. Finally."

"Are you planning on taking a date other than Jack?"

Lorelei shot Vivi a look, but Vivi just shrugged.

"It's a fair question. Seating charts do need to be made."

Argh. Lorelei closed her eyes and rubbed her temples. "I'm going stag. You'll just have to entertain me during dinner."

"Are you sure there's no one else you'd like to invite?"

What a loaded question. "Nah."

"'Nah?' That's your answer?"

Lorelei nodded and stroked the silk sarong again.

Vivi arched an eyebrow at her. "You are a really bad liar. You know that, right?"

She should have known better than to try. "There's a guy, but…"

That got her sister's attention. Vivi nudged Lorelei's feet until she curled them up and sat on the other end of the chaise. "My sources here must be falling down on the job. How'd I not know this? How long has this been going on?"

The brief spark of satisfaction that she'd gotten *something* by her sister was muted by the situation itself. "A few weeks. We kept it very quiet and very casual. Which turned out to be a good thing, because it didn't work out. So even if I wanted to ask him I can't."

"Hang on. Back this up. Start with his name."

She could trust Vivi, she knew that, but it was still difficult. Unfortunately it wouldn't get any easier, because she knew Vivi, and the chances of her getting out of this room without divulging the information were slim to none.

She took a deep breath and blew it out. "Donovan St. James."

Even Vivi, who had a game face like no other, couldn't hide her shock. "Whoa! *Really?*"

"Really." She shrugged. "Hard to believe, huh?"

"I would not have ever thought to put you two together, but—"

"I know. I was crazy. But, like I said, it's over."

"Why?"

"Donovan decided that I was ashamed to be seen with him and refused to be my 'dirty little secret' any longer."

"Why would he think you were ashamed of him?"

It was the issue she'd been arguing with herself over for days now. She had to admit the truth. "'Cause I was."

Vivi's jaw dropped in horror. "Lorelei Lucienne LaBlanc, tell me you are kidding."

"I wish I could." She dropped her head back and pulled a pillow over her face. "It's a big mess."

Vivi pulled the pillow away. She did not look happy, either. "Obviously. Now, please continue."

"I got totally hammered at your reception." Vivi's eyes narrowed in disapproval. "And spent the night with him. It just kind of went from there. A little fling."

"Keep talking. You're still not to the 'ashamed of him' part."

Lorelei hated being put on the defensive like this. "You can't deny that if I suddenly announced I was dating Donovan St. James heads all over the Garden District wouldn't explode."

"I won't deny that. But that doesn't make the exploding heads right, either."

"I worked so hard for months, trying to get people to take me seriously—"

"What for?"

Lorelei sighed. "Vivi, *cherie,* I love you, but being your sister really sucks sometimes."

Vivi nodded in understanding and reached out to squeeze her knee. "I know. And I'm sorry."

"I just wanted people to see *me* for once, to take me seriously, and you being gone was the perfect opportunity for that. I've been working toward a goal, and it was finally in reach. Everyone was so happy that I was finally acting like a LaBlanc. Mom and Dad were so proud, new opportunities were coming my way...there's no way I could drop the Donovan bombshell on all of that. I had too much at risk, too much to lose. So, no, I didn't want anyone to know. I was ashamed of myself, of him, of what we were doing..." She dropped her head back again. "It doesn't really matter. It wouldn't have worked out anyway."

"I don't know. Like I said, I never would have thought to put you two together, but now that I do think about it I can totally see it."

That had her sitting upright again. "What?"

"I, too, had my reservations about Donovan, but after I got to know him a little I got past all that. Connor's done work with him, I've sat with him on boards—hell, we invited him to the wedding. You don't see people's heads exploding, do you?"

"They are—just not where you can see. You and Connor can do whatever you want. You're established and way too powerful to mess with. No one would ever risk taking you two on. Now, me? I may be a LaBlanc, but I'm not... Well, that's just a whole different story."

Vivi was shaking her head. "You are not just a LaBlanc. You're Lorelei LaBlanc. Unique, fantastic and the envy of many. Including me, sometimes. Nothing will change that, and I never knew you thought there was some standard to meet or mold to fit in order to be judged worthy of something. I'm glad you're feeling stronger and more sure of yourself. I'm glad that others are finally starting to realize how awesome you are. But you should never distrust yourself or deny your own happiness because you're worried about what others think of you."

It was an impassioned speech, one that made her feel proud and loved, but Vivi wasn't exactly the audience she sought to impress. "Thanks. I'll keep that in mind for next time."

"Why wait until next time? It's obvious you really like Donovan. You wouldn't be so miserable otherwise."

"At first it was just hormones and chemistry and sex, but, then… Yeah." She'd been refusing to admit it to herself, but she couldn't deny it any longer. Good God, she was such a bad liar she couldn't even lie to herself. "I'm crazy about him. I just didn't realize that until after."

"And you haven't talked to him? Apologized and tried to explain?"

"No. I'm not a glutton for punishment."

"And you think it's too late now?"

"I guess it's never too late for an apology, but I don't think it can be fixed. It started off in the wrong place and just kind of stayed there. And I did say some really mean things. So did he, of course. Not all of which were untrue. But it leads me to believe that while he may want me, he doesn't really like me all that much. I'm not the only one who considered this a dirty little secret." That hurt to admit, but if she were going to be really honest with herself, she needed to face all the facts. "Maybe it's better to just let it go."

It was Vivi's turn to sigh. "I wish you'd told me about your grand plan sooner. I could have made things a lot simpler for you."

"I know, but I wanted to do this myself."

"And Donovan?"

"I think that was just doomed from the beginning."

"I don't think it was or is necessarily doomed, but I will respect your decision. Just know that whatever you decide, I've totally got your back. Nobody messes with my little sister."

It was a strong, comforting statement from someone she loved and respected. But she didn't need—didn't *want*—Vivi to fight her battles for her.

Especially since the battle seemed lost already.

The following Wednesday, Donovan picked up a newspaper on the way home. His oldest niece had placed second in the city-wide spelling bee and, according to the excited text he'd received that morning, a picture of the top three with their trophies was in the "Wednesday Pages."

He got himself a drink and unfolded the paper. The glossy society magazine slid out. On the front there was a picture of Michael LaBlanc, Lorelei's father, and a headline about his retirement. *The big bash,* he thought. *Lorelei's big moment.*

He flipped through, scanning, looking for the spelling bee, and ran straight into the write-up of the LaBlanc party with full-color pictures. A group picture of Lorelei's parents, two other older couples he assumed were business partners, Connor and Vivi—and Lorelei. Lorelei looked regal in a silver and black cocktail dress, her hair pulled up to show off her elegant features—the image hit him hard.

So hard, in fact, he didn't see Jack Morgan hovering over Lorelei's shoulder like the Hindenburg at first. It seemed Lorelei had buckled under the pressure after all and let herself be paired off with her mother's Mr. Right selection.

"Way to stand strong, Princess."

He turned the page. They deserved each other. As he located the picture of his niece he thought of the invitation that had arrived yesterday, inviting him to a party at ConMan Studios exclusively for the donors to Connor's pet charities like the Children's Music Project.

That was going to be awkward. Connor and Vivi must not know about his and Lorelei's little fling or else he wouldn't have received an invitation, donor or not. He knew he wouldn't extend an invite if the roles were reversed.

He had to assume Jack would be there—even if, as Lorelei claimed, he'd donated pocket change. It had been bad enough watching Jack hover over her previously, but now…?

Even as angry as he was, he still felt the loss of Lorelei like a knife in his gut. The one thing he'd come to realize recently was that the hurt ran deep because he'd allowed himself to get used to her. The anger was much easier to deal with than the betrayal and hurt, so he focused on that.

Lorelei's complete disappearance from his life only proved his accusations correct. And she'd very obviously moved on; he hadn't heard anything from her since the night she'd left. Based on that picture, she wasn't exactly suffering from the loss.

He'd wanted to call her; he nearly had a dozen times. But he'd finally deleted her number from his phone to remove the temptation altogether. He wanted her. He missed her. No one made him laugh—or jerked his chain—quite like Lorelei. He hadn't realized how used he'd become to having her around until she wasn't there, and his house felt a little empty. So did his bed.

There was also an empty, hollow place in his stomach.

He might as well accept the facts. Lorelei lived in a different world, and that world had no place and no tolerance for him. And since she wasn't willing to jeopardize her place in that world for him… Yeah, he just needed to accept that. Acceptance would help him move on. Move past Lorelei. His brain was on board for that, but getting his heart and body to agree was tough.

Lesson learned. Move on.

He thought about that for a minute, then grabbed his phone and called Jess.

CHAPTER TEN

LORELEI WAS ABOUT to pull her hair out. Someone needed to explain to Connor that the title "rock god" was not literal. He could *not* simply decide to throw a major party for over a hundred people and assume it would simply come to pass because he wanted it to.

Obviously Connor thought that catering just *happened*.

She was in the uncomfortable position of being both family and employee. The employee wanted to quit in a fully deserved huff, but as family, she hadn't quite ruled out strangling him in his sleep. The only thing keeping her from doing either was her pride and the fact that Vivi would probably be mad at her. *LaBlancs love a challenge. This is just a challenge.*

This event was going to happen one way or the other, by God—even if Lorelei had to call in every favor she'd ever been owed. Pride was definitely driving her. She was a LaBlanc, and party planning and hostessing were in her DNA. She'd peel the crawfish herself before she let this event be anything but perfect.

However, deep down she was rather glad she had plenty to focus on and frustrate her. She'd been thinking about calling Donovan, going to see him—*something*—just to see if there was a way to repair the damage, but she'd chickened out every time. It had been a tough couple of weeks. Callie's romance had flamed out and she was around a lot more, alternating between feeling sorry for herself and cursing her ex's name. Since Callie had no idea that Lorelei had ever been with Donovan in the first place, Lorelei had to suck it up and pretend everything was just fine instead of joining her in misery.

Pretending was very hard to do, since she missed Donovan like crazy. She kept picking up her phone to call or text him random things, but then she'd remember that look on Donovan's face and remember she couldn't do that anymore. And it made her sad. He'd been the one person who'd been there for her through all of this, and now that she had accomplished her goal she didn't really have anyone to share it with who could really appreciate it.

So the party was a good thing. Focusing on it, however frustrating, was actually keeping her sane. Or sane-ish.

But tonight would definitely be a test. She'd designed and ordered the invitations, but the receptionist had been the one to get the guest list, mail the invitations and record the RSVPs. She hadn't even thought to look at the list until yesterday.

She'd been prepared to see Donovan's name on the list. She hadn't been prepared to see him RSVP in the positive, though. And she'd *really* been unprepared to see that he'd included a plus-one.

That had been a bit of a blow.

Obviously she'd left and he'd simply called, "Next!" She told herself she shouldn't be surprised, but it still hurt. The fling that wasn't supposed to be anything had turned into something. At least for her. She'd just realized it a little too late. After all that time worrying about what other people would think, she now only cared what one person thought.

It didn't seem as if he was thinking about *her* much at

all. She wished she could say the same. It had been the sight of "and guest" that had driven a hard piece of knowledge home: she was in love with Donovan St. James.

Unfortunately she'd come to that realization only after it was too late.

And now she'd have to face him—and the woman he'd replaced her with so quickly—and not let that knowledge show. It was a challenge she was not looking forward to.

Lorelei made one last check of the studio's reception area. The scent of fresh flowers filled the room. Caterers were setting up appetizer stations, and bartenders in matching uniforms looked ready to go. A loop of recordings made here, at ConMan, over the last few months played softly over the speakers. Security was already watching the doors, and Connor and Vivi were sneaking in one last canoodle in the sound booth before the guests began arriving.

Everything was as ready as it could be.

Except for her. She still needed to change and gather herself.

Upstairs, in Connor and Vivi's bedroom, Lorelei slipped into her new dress. It was a beautiful deep scarlet that showed plenty of leg and quite a bit of cleavage. It would be totally inappropriate in most settings, but tonight she was here as Connor's assistant, not Vivi's stand-in. She could go a *little* wilder, and after weeks of guarding herself, it felt quite good to let a little bit of her back out.

And it gave her confidence. Confidence she was really going to need if Donovan was going to be here. With a date.

That knowledge made her take a few extra minutes touching up her make-up and hair. After slipping on her shoes, she stood in front of the mirror and examined herself critically from every angle. It would have to do. She took a deep breath and braced herself.

The elevator had to be turned off during the party, so Lorelei came down the back stairs through Connor's office and into the crowded reception area. *Wow.* How long had she been gone? Hadn't these people ever heard of being fashionably late? A quick look around told her that everything seemed to be under control, so now she needed to mingle and make nice with the guests.

She felt a hand at her elbow. Vivi was pulling her back into Connor's office.

"I need to tell you something."

"What?" she said as Vivi shut the door behind them.

"Donovan's here—"

"I know. I can—"

"With Jessica Reynald."

That was a real blow to her ego. She swallowed hard. Somehow that seemed personal, although rationally she knew it couldn't be. "Thanks for the heads up."

"It gets better." Vivi's tone did not match her words, and Lorelei braced herself. "Jack just arrived."

"I knew he would. I can't seem to shake him off."

"You're going to have to be clear and direct."

That was the same thing Donovan had said. "But just not here, not tonight, in front of all these people."

Vivi frowned. "I'm pretty sure he's doing it on purpose. On the other hand…" She paused and brushed Lorelei's hair back over her shoulders. "Having Jack around might counterbalance Donovan and his date."

"I'm okay, really. He's moved on. I get that. I'm an adult and I can handle it."

"I know you can." Vivi squeezed her shoulders in support, then opened the door. Music and conversation rushed in to fill the silence.

For the next forty-five minutes Lorelei worked the crowd with every ounce of energy and personality she possessed. Connor had three pet projects, all music-related, and this crowd was the money that funded them and the talent that supported them. The energy in the room was amazing. So much talent, a shared love of music—and, of course, the money that supported these and other projects. Lorelei couldn't quite quell the rather hollow feeling in her stomach and the dread that sat on her shoulders, but she was able to hold it at bay and put on a good game face.

Then she turned and found herself face-to-face with Donovan. Her stomach tied itself into a knot, but she forced the smile to stay steady and even. Donovan wasn't alone, and she would not make a scene. Even if it killed her.

"Glad you could come, Donovan."

"I wouldn't have missed it for the world."

He introduced her to the people in his group: the front man of a zydeco band whose Cajun accent was so thick he was barely understandable, a white-haired blues guitarist who looked to be about a hundred years old, and a tall, sultry jazz singer who made her feel downright dowdy. Jessica, she noted, was nowhere around.

The presence of the others made it a little easier, but every time she looked at Donovan, her heart ached a little. When he laughed, it made the knot in her stomach tighten. She concentrated on being a good hostess, participating in the conversation, but she was dying a bit inside. Donovan's eyes were uninterested; they flicked over her and then dismissed her. There was no special, knowing smirk on his face.

She'd been right not to call him. It was bad enough coming to terms with that here, where he couldn't actually say anything to make her feel worse.

Was that even possible?

"Could you all excuse me? I need to check on a few things." It was a perfectly normal excuse for someone in her position to make, but she felt like a coward as she retreated. A relieved coward, and one who needed a break, but a coward nonetheless.

Just in case anyone was watching, Lorelei gave a cursory glance over the food and made sure that there were no empty dishes or dirty glassware sitting about, but the catering staff were on top of things and there was nothing really for her to do. She got a club soda from the bartender and stepped back near the fichus tree, out of sight, for a small breather.

There was a couple on the other side. The woman had her back turned, so Lorelei couldn't tell who she was, but Troy, one of the sound engineers, was definitely flirting.

She silently wished Troy luck as she started to move away and give them some privacy, but the name "Donovan" froze her feet in place. A split-second later she recognized the woman's voice: Jessica.

"I'm just arm candy. When Donovan called, he said he needed company. I wasn't about to turn down a chance to come to this party."

Feeling silly, Lorelei took a step back to hear better.

"I do *not* want to get on Donovan St. James's bad side," Troy said.

Smart man.

"All he has is a bad side right now. He's grumpy and angry at something."

That might be my fault.

"Even if he hadn't made it very clear I was just here to look pretty," Jessica continued, "he's so foul-tempered I nearly backed out."

"I'm glad you didn't." Troy was definitely moving in, hoping to score.

"Me, too."

Troy lowered his voice then, and Lorelei couldn't hear what he said next, but she'd lost interest anyway. That changed *everything.* Donovan hadn't turned straight to Jessica to replace her; he hadn't brought her as anything more than a showpiece.

To make her jealous, maybe?

That knot in her stomach released a tiny bit.

The foul mood was probably her fault, but it could easily mean he was just still angry over the whole mess. She could hold out the hope that maybe, *maybe,* he was a little miserable, too. That maybe he felt the same way about her that she felt about him.

That gave her hope.

And since Jessica wasn't really in the picture she had no ethical reason not to suck it up and apologize. She wouldn't be poaching on anyone else's turf.

With all these people around Donovan wouldn't— or *probably* wouldn't—make a stink if she told him she wanted to speak with him privately, and Connor's office would be private enough…

I'm going to do it. She had no idea what she was going to say, but she'd think on her feet, make it up as she went along. As long as she was honest, she had to believe the right words would come.

It was a big risk, but it was a risk worth taking. She had no idea what Donovan would say, but she had no problem groveling if she had to. She just wanted him, and she'd suffer whatever humiliation he wanted to dish out as her penance.

And if it was too late? The damage too extensive? She

didn't want to think about that. It would make this harder, but LaBlancs didn't back down from a challenge.

She actually felt better than she had in days. Her chest felt lighter, her head clearer. Quietly easing out from behind the fichus, she handed her glass to the surprised-looking bartender and scanned the room, looking for Donovan.

She thought she heard his voice and spun around—right into the waiting hands of Jack.

"Hey, sweetheart, I've been looking all over for you."

Oh, *merde.*

Donovan regretted giving in to the impulse to bring Jess. After less than an hour, she'd informed him that his attitude sucked, and if he was going to be grumpy and evil, he would have to do it without her on his arm. *She* was going to go and find people who actually wanted to enjoy themselves. He hadn't seen her since, but he really couldn't blame her.

He really had no reason to be at a party. Even a good party like this one. *Especially* this party. It might be Connor's name on the invitation, but this had Lorelei's stamp all over it, which only added to his already evil mood.

He shouldn't have come at all. He could have declined. He just hadn't realized how petty he actually was. He'd known Lorelei would be here, and with all the maturity of a ten-year-old, had decided he'd show her how little it had all meant by showing up at her party and being just damn fine. Bringing Jess had been to rub it in.

He hadn't counted on the plan backfiring on him. He might be putting on the face of being fine, but Lorelei was reveling in it. She circulated like a social butterfly, a huge smile on her face. That smile had been muted slightly when she'd put in her appearance in front of him, as required by the rules of etiquette, but no one, not even him, would be able to tell that they'd ever been more than polite acquaintances.

That had only made his bad mood worse. That red dress had every one of her curves on tasteful display, and the sound of her voice had stoked him like a furnace. He'd been soaking up her presence like a thirsty plant in a rainstorm as she charmed everyone in the crowd, then been left unsatisfied as she moved on.

And it wasn't as if he could ignore her. Whether it was that dress, or the sound of her voice or something more intangible, he could feel her in the room, and he found himself looking for her out of the corner of his eye.

This time when he located her, she was in Jack's arms. The feeling he now recognized as jealousy clawed at his guts. He was going to have to recommend that St. James Media find a new law firm to represent them, because he was *not* going to be gracious about this.

Jess could stay if she wanted to; *he* would probably be better served by getting the hell out of here. He scanned the crowd to see where Jess was, and his eyes landed on Lorelei and Jack again. Only this time Jack was wearing a frown instead of that possessive, smug smile. Lorelei also looked peeved, and her eyes kept darting around as if she was trying to make sure no one was watching them. It was definitely one of those whispering-type fights. *Trouble in paradise already.* He couldn't dredge up much sympathy, though.

Jack reached for her hand and Lorelei snatched it back. "Damn it, Jack, *no*."

The fact Lorelei was shouting was almost as shocking as her words. Heads started to turn in her direction.

"You're not listening to me. I'm in love with someone else!"

All conversation in the room stopped. Every eye in the room focused on Lorelei, who went from angry to horrified in under three seconds. Her face turned the color of her dress as she realized what she'd done.

Donovan's shock at Lorelei's shout had delayed his brain in the processing of her words. When they finally registered, he thought his heart might have stopped beating. *Love.* That happy, content feeling he'd had was love—and the hollow, achy feeling in his stomach now was him suffering because she didn't love him and had left him. The feelings were so alien and strange he hadn't realized what they were, but now he did. The big question was whether the "someone else" was him...

Someone coughed in the silence.

Jack looked caught at the apex of anger, humiliation and disappointment. When he felt the attention of the room on him, he quickly tried to reschool his face into something more blasé and amused. He failed. Donovan had no pity for him.

There was movement in the crowd, and he saw Vivi dodging between people into the clearing that had opened around Lorelei and Jack.

Then, as if someone had sent out a signal, the conversation started again—not at its previous volume, but everyone seemed to be trying to pretend the last endless minute hadn't happened.

"Wait."

Eyes focused inward, Lorelei spoke softly. He'd have missed it if he hadn't been frozen in place himself, watching her.

She inhaled and tried again. "Excuse me."

This time her voice carried and that total silence cloaked the room again.

Lorelei swallowed hard. "First, let me apologize for that

outburst. I really do try to avoid making a scene and embarrassing people. Especially myself." She smiled weakly. "But, since I brought everyone into this, you deserve to hear the rest of it."

She turned to Jack. "I'm sorry, Jack, but you just weren't taking the hint. I didn't mean to break it to you quite like that."

Jack shrugged, obviously wishing he was anywhere but here. Lorelei addressed the crowd again.

"And, again, I apologize to y'all for interrupting your evening. But, since Vivi is probably going to kill me for making a scene tonight," she joked, "I have something I need to say before she does."

Lorelei's eyes found Donovan's in the crowd.

"I've been a real brat. And my priorities have been way out of whack. I have no excuse other than that I had my sights set on a goal and I totally forgot to look around me at anything else."

Others had noticed Lorelei's stare and followed it. A path began to open between them as people stepped back, and Donovan could feel the weight of their eyes on him. But Lorelei had him hypnotized again, and he couldn't break free.

"I wanted respect. I wanted people to see me as not just Vivi's little sister. The first person who did, though…" She sighed. "I didn't quite see *him*. And that was wrong. Even when he pointed it out to me I still missed it. He had—and has—every right to be angry with me. I should have said this already, but I didn't have the guts. I'm so sorry, Donovan."

He managed a nod.

Lorelei's lips stretched into a shaky smile. "And I realize it was probably kind of sudden and, um, not *quite* the way one is supposed to announce those kinds of things, but it's true. I'm in love...with you."

His heart felt as if it would burst in his chest, and it was hard to breathe.

There was an audible *"aww"* around him, as if someone had cued up a sound effect, and every single person in the room looked at him. It was obviously his move, but he didn't quite have full motor control yet.

As the silence stretched out, he saw Lorelei's smile start to waver.

Once again, Lorelei was able to tie his tongue, but he was able to get his feet moving. Lorelei's smile grew a bit stronger once he moved toward her, but it was still wary. Standing in front of her, he couldn't figure out what he wanted to say. He did the only thing he could do, the thing he'd been wanting to do: pulled her into his arms. She came willingly, easily, and her mouth landed on his with a power and promise that weakened his knees.

Vaguely he heard cheers and applause, but the only thing that registered was the feel of Lorelei melting into him, making him feel whole. He knew what that speech had cost her, and he loved her all the more for making it anyway.

Someone cleared her throat. "Might I suggest you finish your conversation somewhere private?" Vivi asked. "Connor's office is available."

Lorelei flushed and looked embarrassed, but she nodded at her sister. Twining her fingers through his, she tugged gently. "This way."

In the quiet semi-darkness of Connor's office, he finally found his voice again. "You made a bit of a scene there."

"I know."

"What are all those people going to think?"

She grabbed the lapels of his jacket and walked backward, towing him toward Connor's desk. She boosted herself up and pulled him close. "I honestly do not care."

His hands went to her waist as he stepped between her legs. The hem of her dress slid dangerously up her thighs. "Really?"

She tipped her face up for another kiss. "Really."

"Surely you care just a little bit?" he teased.

She shook her head. "I set out to prove people wrong, and I've accomplished that. I wanted to change their minds, and though you say that's not possible—and you might be right—I finally realized I honestly don't care. What can they do to me that's worse than what I've already done to myself?"

"And what *did* you do to yourself?"

"I drove you away." She shrugged. "I know that's technically considered something done to you, but I've been pretty miserable about it. I don't even *want* to be a junior member of the Women's Auxiliary Guild, so it hardly seemed right that I'd have to sacrifice you to gain it." Her hands rested on his shoulders, her fingers idly caressing the back of his neck as she spoke. Then her fingers stilled. "I am really sorry."

"Me, too. I changed the rules in the middle of the game and expected you to play. And then I got mad when you didn't. You were right about me. I am a pompous, blowhard jerk."

That earned him a grin. "And I'm just the bratty princess to handle you."

An eyebrow went up in challenge.

"If you're willing to give this another shot, that is. A proper one this time."

He inhaled, letting her scent curl through him. Meeting her eyes evenly, he said the one thing he'd been trying to deny this whole time. "I love you, Lorelei." Saying it out loud made it real—and a little scary. But he wasn't worried that he might have the emotion wrong: his whole body felt better and his mind felt clearer once he said it.

"And I love you."

All the things he'd set out to accomplish and prove in his life paled in comparison to knowing that Lorelei loved him. "I just wish you'd told me *before* you told the rest of New Orleans."

She pretended to think. "There are a *few* people who still don't know. I'll work on that tomorrow."

"There's a reporter for the paper out there."

"I know. Evelyn Jones. The same woman who speculated about my bad behavior with you before. She must be feeling quite vindicated at the moment." Lorelei bit her lip and let her hands slide down his chest toward his belt buckle. "Maybe we should *really* give her something to talk about…"

EPILOGUE

IT WAS A SMALL crowd—just their families and a few friends. Less than fifty people, total. Lorelei had been to bigger children's birthday parties.

She wore white, because that was what brides wore, but the dress was neither pouffy nor big—just a simple sheath. Vivi was her only attendant, and she looked elegant and ethereal in silvery-blue. Both Donovan's brothers had stood up with him, making the numbers uneven, but it didn't really matter to anyone except the photographer, who kept grumbling that the pictures would be asymmetrical.

Connor had laughed when she'd asked to use the studio for her wedding, but she'd thrown enough parties here that it was where she felt most comfortable. It had taken a while for her family to get over the fact that Lorelei didn't want to get married in the cathedral with half of the city in attendance—especially since she would have had to invite a bunch of people who would be *tsk*ing under their breath the whole time because she was marrying outside of the fold.

Not that she cared what they thought or what they said, but she wasn't going to feed them while they shook their heads and whispered about her.

Plus, she was sentimental enough to want to make it

permanent in the same space where she'd admitted to Donovan that she loved him for the first time.

So this wedding was exactly what she wanted—from the small guest list to the simple flowers and all of Donovan's favorite foods. Food had been the only thing Donovan expressed a preference on—he'd wanted to elope to Vegas, and when she nixed that idea he'd taken over the menu. It wasn't your normal wedding reception food, but she didn't care.

Lorelei's cheeks hurt from smiling so much, but they weren't fake smiles worn for the crowd. She was just happy.

Donovan was on one of the sofas, talking to his brother, but when she joined them, Matt excused himself. She leaned against Donovan's broad chest and sighed.

"Everything okay?"

"Everything's perfect. Just resting my feet for a second."

"When will you learn not to wear shoes that kill your feet?"

She extended one leg to examine her shoes. She'd painted her toenails the same silvery-blue as Vivi's dress. "But they're so pretty." When Donovan raised an eyebrow at her, she confessed, "I have flats in my bag if I need them. I've learned my lesson well."

He took her hand and twined his fingers through hers. "Your grandmother is not happy."

"I'm the first LaBlanc not to marry in the cathedral in like a hundred years. Of course she's not happy about that. She's not convinced this is truly legit."

Donovan sighed. "We're going to have to go see the priest and get this blessed or something, aren't we?"

"Only if I hope to be in the will." The background

music stopped at the same time the buzz of conversation did, and Lorelei looked around. "What's going on?"

In answer to her question, she saw Connor seated at the piano.

Donovan stood and held out a hand. "How badly do your feet hurt?"

"They're okay."

"Good. Because we're supposed to dance now."

She let Donovan lead her to the middle of the room as Connor played the opening bars of one of his songs. It seemed it was rather handy having a brother-in-law who was a rock star.

As always, it felt good—and right—to be held against Donovan's chest. She could feel the beat of his heart, and that special smell of him filled her lungs as she inhaled.

"Always remember..." Connor sang, and Lorelei couldn't imagine a more perfect moment. *"You and me, and the magic of this day."*

The hand on her lower back moved gently in time with the music, keeping her close, making her feel safe.

"Today I'm giving you my heart."

She looked up at Donovan. "I did that a while ago."

His smile made her heart flip over. "I know. This just makes it legal."

"Today I'm giving you my love.
Today I'm giving you my all.
Promise me, you'll save me..."

"I love you, Lorelei St. James."

"Lorelei St. James." It still felt a little funny to say it, but… "I kinda like the sound of that."

"Today I'm giving you my hand.
Today we'll say 'I do.'
So always remember..."

She chuckled and Donovan looked at her. "What?"

"It still bums me out a little that I don't remember our first night together."

"You'll have to trust me when I tell you that it wasn't our best effort. All the nights you do remember are *way* better."

"What about tonight?"

The look Donovan gave her should have melted her on the spot. "Oh, tonight's going to be amazing. Definitely one to remember. Are you up to it?"

"Are you kidding me? I may be a St. James now, but I'm still a LaBlanc. And LaBlancs *love* a challenge." She rose up on her tiptoes. "But more than any challenge, I love *you.*"

* * * * *

ROMANCE

Playing the Dutiful Wife	Carol Marinelli
The Fallen Greek Bride	Jane Porter
A Scandal, a Secret, a Baby	Sharon Kendrick
The Notorious Gabriel Diaz	Cathy Williams
A Reputation For Revenge	Jennie Lucas
Captive in the Spotlight	Annie West
Taming the Last Acosta	Susan Stephens
Island of Secrets	Robyn Donald
The Taming of a Wild Child	Kimberly Lang
First Time For Everything	Aimee Carson
Guardian to the Heiress	Margaret Way
Little Cowgirl on His Doorstep	Donna Alward
Mission: Soldier to Daddy	Soraya Lane
Winning Back His Wife	Melissa McClone
The Guy To Be Seen With	Fiona Harper
Why Resist a Rebel?	Leah Ashton
Sydney Harbour Hospital: Evie's Bombshell	Amy Andrews
The Prince Who Charmed Her	Fiona McArthur

MEDICAL

NYC Angels: Redeeming The Playboy	Carol Marinelli
NYC Angels: Heiress's Baby Scandal	Janice Lynn
St Piran's: The Wedding!	Alison Roberts
His Hidden American Beauty	Connie Cox

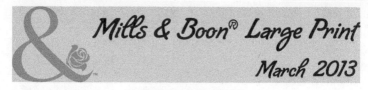

Mills & Boon® Large Print

March 2013

ROMANCE

A Night of No Return	Sarah Morgan
A Tempestuous Temptation	Cathy Williams
Back in the Headlines	Sharon Kendrick
A Taste of the Untamed	Susan Stephens
The Count's Christmas Baby	Rebecca Winters
His Larkville Cinderella	Melissa McClone
The Nanny Who Saved Christmas	Michelle Douglas
Snowed in at the Ranch	Cara Colter
Exquisite Revenge	Abby Green
Beneath the Veil of Paradise	Kate Hewitt
Surrendering All But Her Heart	Melanie Milburne

HISTORICAL

How to Sin Successfully	Bronwyn Scott
Hattie Wilkinson Meets Her Match	Michelle Styles
The Captain's Kidnapped Beauty	Mary Nichols
The Admiral's Penniless Bride	Carla Kelly
Return of the Border Warrior	Blythe Gifford

MEDICAL

Her Motherhood Wish	Anne Fraser
A Bond Between Strangers	Scarlet Wilson
Once a Playboy…	Kate Hardy
Challenging the Nurse's Rules	Janice Lynn
The Sheikh and the Surrogate Mum	Meredith Webber
Tamed by her Brooding Boss	Joanna Neil

Mills & Boon® Hardback
April 2013

ROMANCE

Master of her Virtue	Miranda Lee
The Cost of her Innocence	Jacqueline Baird
A Taste of the Forbidden	Carole Mortimer
Count Valieri's Prisoner	Sara Craven
The Merciless Travis Wilde	Sandra Marton
A Game with One Winner	Lynn Raye Harris
Heir to a Desert Legacy	Maisey Yates
The Sinful Art of Revenge	Maya Blake
Marriage in Name Only?	Anne Oliver
Waking Up Married	Mira Lyn Kelly
Sparks Fly with the Billionaire	Marion Lennox
A Daddy for Her Sons	Raye Morgan
Along Came Twins…	Rebecca Winters
An Accidental Family	Ami Weaver
A Date with a Bollywood Star	Riya Lakhani
The Proposal Plan	Charlotte Phillips
Their Most Forbidden Fling	Melanie Milburne
The Last Doctor She Should Ever Date	Louisa George

MEDICAL

NYC Angels: Unmasking Dr Serious	Laura Iding
NYC Angels: The Wallflower's Secret	Susan Carlisle
Cinderella of Harley Street	Anne Fraser
You, Me and a Family	Sue MacKay

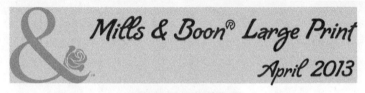

ROMANCE

A Ring to Secure His Heir	Lynne Graham
What His Money Can't Hide	Maggie Cox
Woman in a Sheikh's World	Sarah Morgan
At Dante's Service	Chantelle Shaw
The English Lord's Secret Son	Margaret Way
The Secret That Changed Everything	Lucy Gordon
The Cattleman's Special Delivery	Barbara Hannay
Her Man in Manhattan	Trish Wylie
At His Majesty's Request	Maisey Yates
Breaking the Greek's Rules	Anne McAllister
The Ruthless Caleb Wilde	Sandra Marton

HISTORICAL

Some Like It Wicked	Carole Mortimer
Born to Scandal	Diane Gaston
Beneath the Major's Scars	Sarah Mallory
Warriors in Winter	Michelle Willingham
A Stranger's Touch	Anne Herries

MEDICAL

A Socialite's Christmas Wish	Lucy Clark
Redeeming Dr Riccardi	Leah Martyn
The Family Who Made Him Whole	Jennifer Taylor
The Doctor Meets Her Match	Annie Claydon
The Doctor's Lost-and-Found Heart	Dianne Drake
The Man Who Wouldn't Marry	Tina Beckett